ISBN-13: 978-1475251265
ISBN-10: 1475251262

DUCKPIN HUNT

MARY K. LAVIN

Prologue

The scissors cut around the newspaper article leaving no jagged edges in their wake. The article floated free and hands spread it out on the table to read:

Lester Holmes, age 47, was found dead in a South Baltimore duckpin bowling alley Friday around 9:30 a.m. He was apparently murdered by a blow to the head. His body was placed in the setting machinery of one of the alley's lanes and was discovered by the alley's manager, Ivy Walker, when she tested the machine in the morning. This "duckpin murder" has created alarm in a community that is generally considered safe. Police would not speculate on motives or suspects at this time.

The hands smoothed it over several times, finally folding it into halves and pocketing it.

Chapter One

Sunlight streamed through the window as Dart Hastings hammered away on the computer keyboard putting thoughts into words. Marvin, her rotund orange tabby cat, strolled in and jumped on her lap. He batted at her frizzy red hair which hung down loose around her face. She absentmindedly pulled it back in a ponytail.

Dart lived in a second floor apartment on the cozy side of small. It was located in a rowhouse in an older tree-lined neighborhood a mile or so from downtown Baltimore. It was quiet and safe but did not offer much else. That was fine with Dart. A researcher by trade, a typical day for Dart began with some writing time. Some days might include some interviews, usually by phone or conference call.

It was harder to concentrate this day than others. Dart was nursing a slight headache brought on by a night of celebrating at Ivanhoe's, the local watering hole. An avid duckpin bowler, Dart's team had finished third in the league championship the previous evening at Citylanes, an alley on the city's edge. The night had been eventful from start to finish. Just as she started ruminating once again on the roll that had ended the championship, the phone rang, bringing her back to surface. Dart stretched her tall, lanky frame and reached for the phone.

"Dart, it's Billy Blaze from over at Citylanes. We got big problems over here."

"What's going on, Billy?" Dart asked.

"Just...we got big problems," Billy paused and then said: "Lester's....dead."

Dart was stunned. Lester Holmes was the ringer on "Colleen's Men", the reigning champs in the league. He had just bowled a 135 the previous night and his team had won the championship.

"What happened?" she sputtered to Billy.

"Me and Miss Ivy found him in the lanes when we were setting up this morning. He....he fell right down from lane seven. His head was all gashed in....it was bad. Like being in 'Nam or something. I need some help with Miss Ivy---she's a mess."

Dart told Billy she would head right down and quickly gathered her things together. Driving the route to Citylanes, she thought about poor Miss Ivy. As the manager of Citylanes, Miss Ivy could always been found at her desk her head bent over working out "the numbers" as she called it. Or the accounting of each night's takes. In her tight cursive writing, she diligently kept the books and marked each night's attendance and funds. This would really shake up her world.

Dart pulled up to Citylanes. The harsh light of day made the mid-nineteenth century commercial building look downtrodden. An ambulance and several squad cars were blocking the street. Baltimore was a city used to death but that did not mean a close knit neighborhood like South Baltimore would not feel its impact.

The top two floors of the building had been used as a duckpin alley for sixty years. The entrance was on the side of the building in an alleyway. A policeman stopped her at the entry. She explained she was called to help out. He had her wait as he radioed to someone. Billy Blaze came down within a minute. Not unlike Dart, Billy was a wiry red-head in his late thirties. But they were no relation. He and his identical twin brother, Bobby, were the unofficial ringleaders of the bowling alley.

"Officer," he whined, "I got a seventy five year old woman up there that I need help with. Can you just let her come up so we can get her down together?"

The officer said: "Make it quick."

Dart and Billy headed up the creaking stairwell with its wide wooden treads. Dart caught a whiff of the familiar alley smell---which death had not taken away. Upstairs on the second floor, the scene was swarming with people. The décor of Citylanes had not changed much since its beginnings. To the rear of the alley, there was a soda fountain counter, a shoe room, lockers and a small office. The bulk of the room was comprised of twelve lanes with accompanying seating areas. Spanning the entire sidewall, next to lane one, huge lettering boasted: THIS IS DUCKPIN COUNTRY. Dart's eyes immediately targeted lane seven but all that remained was some procedural equipment. A couple of officials were taking photographs. Lester's body had apparently been removed.

In the middle of all the hub-bub, she spotted Miss Ivy sitting alone. She had her face covered with her hands and was rocking back and forth. Her distinctive "skunk" hairdo stood out in the crowd as usual: a wide swath of white hair surrounded by black. Dart had always assumed she dyed the black and left the front piece white. As Dart and Billy rushed over to her, she looked up and reached for Billy's hand. Her china doll complexion was crumpled with age unlike most other days when it was wreathed in smiles. He immediately leaned over to console her. Dart fleetingly wondered where Bobby, the other twin, was.

6

Billy said: "I gotta get Miss Ivy out of here. I've been interrogated twice and so has she. But they have her on hold. Can you help talk to the cops?" Just as he finished saying this, a detective walked over. He was stocky with a large nose and dark features. Billy was helping Miss Ivy to her feet.

"We can't let Miss Walker go just yet," the detective said firmly.

Dart edged off to his side and said in a low voice: "Look, she's not doing so hot. She has a history of heart problems and we are frankly worried about her. Could you interview her after we get her home?"

"Who are you?" the detective's dark eyes bore into her.

Dart felt unaccountably guilty. "Oh, sorry. I'm Dart Hastings. I'm in the league here and I'm a friend..."she trailed off.

Sighing heavily and blowing air out, he said: "Okay, okay. We will be over in the next two hours. Where does she live?"

Billy, who had been standing within earshot, piped in and said: "She's at 443 Maple, other side of the overpass."

"I know it," the detective said, handing his card to Dart.

She said: "Thanks a lot...uh....," looking down at the card, "Detective Marino."

A uniformed officer called over to the detective. "Marino, Medical Examiner needs you on the phone."

Marino looked at the trio in front of him. "Okay, get her home and I'll be by." Then he squinted his eyes at Dart and pointing his finger, he said: "You were here last night, right? We need to talk too."

"I'll help Billy get Miss Ivy in the car and then come back up."

Marino nodded curtly and moved over to the other side of the room.

Dart and Billy each took one of Miss Ivy's arms and headed out. Miss Ivy was unsteady in her gait and leaning heavily on them for support. They slowly made their way down each stair as Miss Ivy all of sudden stopped. She turned to Dart with unfocused eyes and tears streamed down her face: "Dart, what are we going to do? We got eight lanes reserved for Rock 'N' Bowl tonight!"

Billy comforted her by saying, "Now, now. We'll take care of it. Don't bother yourself."

Dart thought quickly. Rock 'N' Bowl was held at alleys throughout the city as a way to encourage interest in the dying sport of duckpin. Patrons paid one price to bowl until midnight with however many games they could fit in. All lanes were usually reserved by noon the day Rock 'N' Bowl was scheduled. It had been a boon to business for all the alleys and had basically resurrected Citylanes from bankruptcy. They did not want to lose any of their loyal customers.

"I'll tell you what. I'll make all the phone calls to cancel the reservations and get the word out. Okay?" Dart patted Miss Ivy on the back. "Let's get you out to the car then I'll head back in and take care of things."

Miss Ivy shook her head back and forth as they continued down the stairs at a slow pace. She seemed so dazed. Dart and Billy passed concerned looks to each other.

At Billy's car, he gave Dart a set of keys for Citylanes and they worked out a few more details about locking up before he and Miss Ivy departed. Dart went back upstairs where Marino was having a discussion with several others. She caught the tail end of what one of the people in a white lab coat was saying: ".......blunt instrument to the head, trauma caused bleeding which is probable cause of death. He's been dead for six to eight hours.

Chapter Two

Blunt instrument to the head? Dart's mind tried to grapple with the idea that Lester had been murdered. She went over the game last night in her head wondering how the events could have spiraled out of control to the point of murder. Before she could replay in her mind, Marino called out: "Dart Hastings!" She looked up and he motioned for her to come over to one of the curved benches behind one of the lanes. He told her to take a seat.

At any other time, she would have felt right at home on the bench surrounded by all the beloved sights and smells of the alley. But not this time. She fidgeted nervously with the edge of the bench.

Marino had a pad and licked the tip of a pencil. "Okay, start at the start. What is your connection here?"

Dart explained that she had recently joined the Citylane's league but knew most of the players from her almost lifelong participation in various other city leagues. What she didn't say was how much she loved the sport---and everything that came with it like the garish lighting, the cheap taste of the hot dogs, the flat soda from the fountain and the squeak of the bowling shoes on the lanes.

Marino asked: "Now, let's see....who owns Citylanes?"

"A man named Cal Lombard. I've never met him. I've only been with the league here for about eight months and he's been in the Bahamas the whole time. I gather from Miss Ivy and the others that he's sort of an absentee owner."

"So....Miss Walker stands in for him officially?"

"Miss Ivy pretty much runs the place on her own as best I can tell. This guy, Cal, bought it within the last couple of years. The previous owner and Miss Ivy were pretty tight----maybe extended family or something. Miss Ivy was actually the former women's champion and had held the title for ten consecutive years. When she hurt her back, she became the manager here." Marino's eyes seemed to glaze over a bit with this history.

"What's the connection between Miss Walker and these twins?" As he flipped back through his pad, he said: "Blaze. The Blaze twins."

Dart said: "I don't know the exact financial arrangement but they help her out on a part-time basis. Miss Ivy is generally here during the day and then they

9

show up at night. With some overlap---sometimes she stays during the evening games with them. That was the case last night because she has double duty as the League manager."

"Okay, run through for me what went down here last night." Marino had obviously heard a version of what had gone down. Dart flashed back to the previous evening.

The night had wrapped up thirty five weeks of playing and determined the league champion team and players. As Dart had entered Citylanes, there was tension in the air. The lead teams were "Blaze o' Glory" (the twins' team), "Colleen's Men" (Lester's team) and Dart's team, "Red Fire". Before the game had officially started, there had been plenty of time for the usual teasing back and forth. The easy banter was often initiated by the twins, the ringleaders in the crowd. A lot of it centered around ten-pin jokes such as "Billy's no better than one of those ten pin bowlers" or "Look at Dart hold that ball---she must think it has holes in it or something."

Duckpin had dwindled in popularity since the 1970s and lost more business to ten pin bowling yearly. The sport was based on nine inch pins and small balls with no holes. The nine inch pins were actually shaved down ten pins. The idea had taken off at an alley in downtown Baltimore around the turn of century. It had boomed for many years in the Baltimore area but then lost favor to ten pins-----a fact that galled hard-core duckpin fans.

The first two games of the evening had been uneventful. Dart had played fairly well taking a break in between games for a hot dog and soda. The night had worn on with the usual teasing amongst the teams. The last game had boiled down to Colleen's Men versus the twin's team for first place. Depending on who got first, Dart's team had a chance at vying for second place. However, the twin's team had Bobby who was the top individual bowler in the league. Since their team was most likely to win, Dart's team would be pushed to third or fourth.

A bead of sweat had formed on Dart's upper lip as she concentrated on her rolls with fierce intensity. She was so focused on her game that she had almost missed the situation two lanes over until her teammate, Shirl, had nudged her.

Bobby Blaze was taking his last roll. Lester had already finished his plays and he began heckling Bobby. As Bobby lined up, Lester hissed softly: "Gutter ball....gutter ball."

Bobby threw him a glare and turned back to the lane. As he took a few steps forward and went to release, the hiss of "gutter ball, gutter ball" could be heard again. Bobby faltered and the roll did indeed turn into a gutter ball.

10

Bobby's face turned blood red and he reeled on Lester. "That's not right, Lester," he said in an ice cold voice, "You just don't do that."

Lester laughed at first and then discerned that Bobby wasn't joking around anymore. Lester turned away and headed towards the lockers. Bobby was right on his heels, looming with a strong physical presence. Lester had changed his shoes and tried to speak once more to Bobby. Bobby just shook his head and then violently slammed his locker door. Then he yelled: "It's just not right!"

Lester had left the alley at that point. The atmosphere of fun and good times had been abruptly terminated and everyone had felt the sting of Bobby's final gutter ball.

Dart relayed the high points to Marino and ended with "....so 'Colleen's Men' took the trophy and the money."

"Wait a minute..." Marino stopped Dart. "What money?"

Dart explained to him that the money accumulated in a pot and was collected every week of play. There was a complicated odds system that was difficult to grasp especially since it changed with every shift of rank in the teams.

"So how much did Lester win?"

"Well, first and foremost, he made Bobby lose a rank that he has had for I don't know how long. And then the money on top of that....."

"How much?"

"About three hundred or so...."

"People have killed for less," Marino muttered to himself. "Okay, let's see...." he tapped his pencil against the pad. "Lester Holmes....what do you know about him?"

"To be honest, not much." Dart's thoughts drifted to her last glimpse of Lester. He had been a short, wiry man with jet black hair greased back. He had not been known for his chattiness although he had occasionally chimed in with a sharp retort in response to any ribbing directed his way. He had most often worn grey polyester pants and a matching shirt slightly reminiscent of a penal institute.

"He did have some faded tattoos on each arm----green with anchors---so I always assumed he had been in the Navy at some point. And, now come to think of it, he worked at an automotive shop with the other guys on his team,

Wallie and Joe. Their team was called "Colleen's Men" but I have no idea who Colleen is."

"Okay, last question. Where were you last night after eleven or so?"

Taken aback, Dart said: "I..I was home. In bed."

"Anyone vouch for that?"

Dart shrugged her shoulders and offered: "Marvin, my cat?"

Marino gave her grimace. He stood up and said: "We may need to talk with you later. Okay?"

"Yeah, right. Got it. Listen....I need to use the office here to cancel reservations for Miss Ivy for tonight's Rock 'N' Bowl."

"You won't be able to get in here until late this afternoon. After that the place is yours. "With that, Marino walked off.

Dart thought about it. That was too long to wait to cancel the reservations. Unless....

She snuck into the small dingy office that was Miss Ivy's home away from home. Despite the upheaval of the investigation, she spotted a notebook labeled "Reservations" sitting right on the top. She grabbed that and also an address book laying next to it just in case.

Chapter Three

Detective Marino was a man in his 40s who had started out as a beat cop and worked his way up to investigator, finally earning a spot in the city's esteemed homicide squad. His no nonsense attitude had earned him quick promotions and the respect of his colleagues. He prided himself in being able to wrap up cases in record time. In his opinion, the duckpin murder was going to be similar to all the other murder cases he had solved. The motive would be based on greed, anger or passion. Or a combination thereof. Marino had learned a lot about the deadly sins through his on the job training.

After leaving Citylanes, he had his work cut out for him. It was pretty clear that he needed to talk to Bobby Blaze. He tracked him down at Crab Alley, the local crab joint in the neighborhood. Hot, steamed crabs were as synonymous to Baltimore as duckpin bowling. Having already met Billy, Marino easily recognized Bobby, a slim man in his late 30s, fair skinned with red hair. Bobby was seated at the end of a table with a group of his buddies. The table was covered with newspapers and festooned with a heap of steamed crabs, mallets, knifes, paper towels and pitchers of beer.

Bobby was daintily tearing at a leg of one of the crustaceans. The others at the table were working in a similar fashion. As Marino stood at the head of the table, conversation ceased and all looked up.

"Bobby Blaze," Marino said, "I'm Detective Marino, here to discuss the death of Lester Holmes."

Bobby gestured to an open chair and said: "Have a seat detective. Real sorry to hear about Lester. You want some crabs? Even though it's May, they're pretty tasty for Gulf crabs."

"Not in the mood, Blaze. Excuse yourself so we can speak in private."

"Okay, okay. Let me just wipe the mustard off," Bobby said referring to the crab guts that were smeared around his lips. While some eschewed the guts, colored a disturbing hue somewhere between green and yellow, others favored them as a taste treat.

Joining Marino at the bar, he wiped his hands on his jeans and then proffered one for Marino to shake. After shaking hands, Marino bluntly said: "What happened between you and Lester last night at Citylanes?"

"You play duckpin, detective?"

"No. You want to answer the question."

Bobby's brow furrowed. "We have a lot of fun playing duckpin down at the 'Lanes. We may give each other a hard time but we all get along. Lester went into some new territory last night."

"New territory?"

"Yeah. He gave me a hard time during my last roll. Broke my concentration. He ended up getting first because of it. It just wasn't right and I told him as much. And he didn't like me calling him out on it I guess. So he left right away before we gave out prizes and everything."

"What kind of prizes?"

"Trophies and the like. And there's a cash kitty that everyone puts in to each game."

"How much money are we talking about?"

"Well, let's see. 'Colleen's Men", that's Lester's team, ended up taking $245 home."

"As a team?"

"Oh, no....each team member gets that much."

"Who keeps track of the money?"

"Miss Ivy being as she's the league manager. This is the way most leagues are run. Nothing unusual about it."

Marino reviewed his notes and saw that this jived with what Dart Hastings had told him. Bobby was unperturbed by Lester's death and did not appear nervous. He was a tough read.

Marino asked about his whereabouts after the game. Bobby claimed to have been with his girlfriend, Rita, from the end of the game through about ten in the morning. Giving Marino a wink, he said he had worked out some bowling frustration. He provided Marino the name, number and address of the lady.

Departing Crab Alley, Marino headed to Miss Ivy's. She lived on a short street of rowhouses set off from the rest of the neighborhood through a combination of train tracks and highway overpasses. Surrounded by industrial activities, the tired houses with their formstone fronts held about a hundred years of stories when they had once been better connected to the neighborhood. The sun cast a shadow across all the houses drawing them even closer together. Ironically, the street boasted one of the neighborhood's precious water views of the Middle Branch.

Billy Blaze answered the door of 443. Marino noted the contrast between the twins. Billy had a softer look about him almost as though his features were smoothed over a bit. Both twins shared an odd trait: they each had one blue eye and one green.

Inside the rowhouse, the first room was filled with trophies from Miss Ivy's glory days to the point of suffocation. Miss Ivy was perched on the edge of the floral chintz couch and seemed less bewildered than earlier in the day.

Marino asked her to repeat the story she had already told a couple of times.

She sighed deeply and then said: "Like I told you before, I got to the 'Lanes early because I wanted to set up for Rock 'N' Bowl. We usually get a real big crowd in and I have to figure out who's in which lane. Billy came in to give me a hand." She turned to Billy and smiled gently at him before continuing. "Like always, we started up the machines to make sure they were setting right. One lane at a time is how we do it. When Billy hit seven, "she faltered then started up again, "Lester came down with the pins. Of course, I didn't know it was Lester right then. Billy tells me to call the po-lice and then runs down the lane. He yelled back at me it was Lester. I said 'what's wrong with him?' I thought maybe he was drunk or something and had crawled up into the machinery....."

Miss Ivy's voice trailed off. Marino said: "Just a few more questions. Tell me what happened last night."

Miss Ivy's faded blue eyes blinked rapidly. "Well, we had the League championship game. I'm the manager of the league so I was there. And....do you need all the names of who was there?"

"No, no, that's okay---we got them earlier. What about the problem with Bobby Blaze and Lester?"

"Oh...that was just a misunderstanding. You know how boys get."

Marino thought to himself "Boys?" She was talking about middle aged men. "Alright, tell me about closing up last night at Citylanes."

"Billy checked on everything and I finished up some bookkeeping. Then we locked all the doors and left."

"What time was that?"

"That woulda been…" she hesitated and then said: "What do you think Billy---about 11?"

Billy nodded in assent. Marino could see there might have been some coaching going on.

"Who has the keys?"

"Besides myself, Billy and Bobby share a set. And the owner, Cal Lombard. And…that's it."

"Do you know how I can get in touch with Lombard?"

"It's not easy----he lives down in the Bahamas most of the time. Just checks in now and then. I never can tell when it will be."

Marino said: "What can you tell me about Lester Holmes?"

Miss Ivy looked askance. "Lester? I don't know. I'd known him a long time. We were never close or anything if that's what you are getting at."

"Did he have any enemies?"

"Enemies? What a question!" Billy rose to calm Miss Ivy down as she appeared visibly flustered. Marino gestured for him to leave her be.

She shook her head and repeated to herself: "Enemies…."

Marino broke in and said: "Look, m 'am. This is standard investigative stuff. I'm just trying to get some ideas about who might have done this."

All three were silent. A grey cat that had been curled up peaceably on the end of the sofa suddenly got up, yawned and stretched.

Marino cleared his throat to break the silence. He sensed the interview was going nowhere fast and decided it was best to cut it off. "Well….I will be in touch."

He could almost feel the relief in the room. He headed towards the door and then stopped. Turning back, he said: "One last thing…what team played on lane seven last night?"

Miss Ivy and Billy looked at each other furtively. Billy coughed a little and then said: "It was 'Blaze 'O' Glory'---my team."

Chapter Four

Dart made her way back to her apartment with her head hurting from the tension of the day. She flipped on the answering machine and flopped down on an easy chair. One message from her mother who demanded a call back. Another automated message from a mortgage solicitor.

Marvin strolled in and meowed for attention. Dart stroked his back while trying to control herself from reaching for a pack of cigarettes she had stashed in one of her desk drawers. She instead grabbed a handful of the espresso coffee beans that had replaced her nicotine addiction. Marvin mewed in complaint that the stroking was interrupted.

Dart pulled out the Citylanes notebook and address book. Looking through the notebook, she immediately realized her mistake. The book only covered the month of April. May must be in another book. Damn! She would have to swing by Citylanes and make the calls that afternoon.

By late afternoon, she headed out. Rock 'N' Bowl did not start until 9 p.m. so she had enough time to make the cancellation calls. Pulling onto Main Street was a different experience than earlier in the day. The place was deserted with just some yellow ticker tape flapping in the breeze to indicate the earlier events. Crossing under it, Dart pulled out the keys Miss Ivy had given her and unlocked the door. Her footsteps rang hollow as she walked up the stairs and she felt her nerve endings stand to attention. Shaking herself a bit, she got to the top landing and opened the interior door. She gasped as she saw a figure hanging on the coat rack and then quickly realized it was only the shadow of somebody's forgotten coat. Heart pounding, she turned on all the lights which boldly exposed all the lanes, lane seven now being empty.

In Miss Ivy's little office, she sat down at the desk and pulled herself in, bumping her knees in the process. Too late she realized the desk was too small for her to do that. She pulled herself back from the desk and sat there. She flipped on the little transistor radio that Miss Ivy kept on a shelf. After switching the dial from Miss Ivy's country western station, the nasally voice of the local D.J., Weasel, came over the airwaves and partially filled the silence. Finally situating herself, she located the right reservation book and reached for the rotary dial phone. She began to make calls while trying to ignore the tomb-like atmosphere.

Halfway down the list, she had managed to contact two live bodies and three machines. She took a time out and stretched her legs out under the desk making the same mistake as her knees butted against the desk underside.

One knee scraped against what felt like a rough piece of paper. She adjusted her knee and again felt it. She bent underneath to examine what was there and found a manila envelope glued or taped to the roof of the desk. She hesitated for only a second and then carefully extracted the envelope ripping it at one of the corners. The envelope had been sealed at one time but was now partially open on its own. Dart pulled out a black and white photograph, yellowed with age. It showed Miss Ivy with a man Dart did not recognize and both were holding trophies. Miss Ivy had one hand placed on the man's arm. The back of the photograph had a date only: "Oct 68".

Feeling guilty, Dart carefully placed the photograph back in the envelope and affixed the tape. It must be someone Miss Ivy had a crush on from back in the day, Dart guessed. She hurriedly completed the calls and then gathered her purse together. Getting up, she started out of the office and then gasped. Billy Blaze was standing in the doorway looking at her.

"Billy!" Dart screeched. "You just scared the bejesus out of me!"

Billy put his hands up. "Hey, hey, don't punch me out or nothing. Just got here and saw the light on in the office. Why are you here?"

"Don't you remember we arranged for me to make the cancellation calls for Rock 'N' Bowl?"

He rubbed his hand over a razor stubbled cheek. "Oh, yeah...there's been so much going on I guess I forgot."

Dart said: "I just finished the calls and I was going to post these signs on the door."

Billy just stood there looking dazed.

"Are you going to hang around here, Billy?"

He sighed. "Yeah, I need to clean up some."

He was making Dart a little nervous. "Okay, well I'm outta here." As she walked out, she felt his eyes on her back. He was probably still in shock from finding the body and didn't know quite what to do with himself, she thought. She then realized he could have walked in when she was looking at the photograph and was glad he had not.

Leaving Citylanes, Dart headed towards the depths of suburbia to visit her mother. She owed her more than a phone call and it was easier to just do it. Widowed several years earlier, Dart's mother, Viola, had purchased a small tract house sold at a bargain rate by a developer trying to unload the most unsellable model in the subdivision.

Whenever she pulled onto the main road of the subdivision, Shady Acres Drive, Dart shuddered at the barrenness. No trees, curbed roadway and silly little houses. After a rocky marital ride with Dick Hastings, her mother had settled in for a stable, albeit boring, lifestyle.

As she got out of her car, Viola came and stood at the doorway. A slender woman in her sixties, Viola's head of hair was perfectly coiffed and dyed an ashy blonde shade. In her younger years, she had reminded some of Tippi Hendren and had capitalized on this image. Viola started talking even before Dart was within earshot.

Dart picked up at "....heard it on the news and couldn't believe it. I have told you about going down in the city at night, over and over again." Without waiting for a reply, she continued the one-sided dialogue until Dart finally put a hand up: "Mom, let me in the house and I will tell you all about it."

Making their way into the living room, Dart took a seat on a plastic covered sofa and kicked off her shoes. Her mother immediately picked them up and placed them neatly by the door, side by side, saying: "What can I get you honey? Some iced tea? Something to eat?"

Dart said: "All of the above."

While her mother bustled about in the kitchen, Dart closed her eyes and let her thoughts swirl around. Within minutes, Viola placed a plate heaped with food in front of Dart on a TV tray and a large frosted glass of iced tea next to it. It had the same effect as smelling salts and Dart perked right up.

Over coleslaw, wings and baked beans, Dart recapped the day for Viola concluding with "so I just left the 'Lanes and drove over here."

"Marino, uh? Where's he from?"

"No idea."

"What's he look like?"

"Well....let's see." Dart munched on a roll while contemplating Detective Marino. "He's obviously Italian. I mean, big nose, dark skinned. Got a pot belly on him. What else? Oh---he has a mole right here." She pointed to her left cheek.

Viola slapped her thigh and said: "I bet he's Betty Marino's oldest son. You know Betty-----one of the ladies I play canasta with down at the hall."

Dart replied: "Was it the mole that gave it away? All I can say is, I hope Betty has more sense of humor than her son for your sake."

Her mother arched her eyebrows and Dart explained: "He just doesn't seem like a fun guy is what I mean."

"Now, Dartie, be open. He might be real nice."

"No match-making! Understood?"

"Who, me?" Viola smiled coyly.

Heading back towards the city from her mother's house, Dart felt restless and unsettled. She drove past her street and kept going to Ivanhoe's. Located on an elevated section of Main, there were good views of the cityscape on the block where Ivanhoe's was located. The downtown buildings lit up at night to form a 3-D collage. Dart could easily make out the Bromo-Seltzer tower outlined in blue light, the Maryland National Bank building with its gilded Art Deco details and the Lego-like Legg Mason Building with its steel grid patterns. Stepping up her pace, she walked by a homeless man in the shadows before reaching the bar entry.

New clientele to Ivanhoe's were usually taken aback upon first walking into the establishment. The bar was back lit with red lights, wall papered in a red brocade style and had red vinyl chairs and red and white checkered tablecloths. The bar menu and décor were all based on the owner's love of horse racing and all of its associations----the color red for instance. There were framed photographs of Pimlico Races on the wall and other memorabilia. The only thing missing was a betting booth which Lou, the owner, often talked about doing one day. Lou had named the bar after a horse that had won big in the 1960s. Supposedly, Lou's winnings that day at the track had funded his entire establishment.

The bar was packed out and Dart squeezed through to get a space at the bar. Most of the crowd was familiar. Many had been at last night's game. A voice called out: "Dart!" She looked down to see Larry, one of her teammates, at the other end of the bar. She made her way through the crowd and overheard snippets of conversation around her. The place was abuzz with talk about Lester's death.

Larry edged over to make room for Dart. He still had his uniform on from his day job at a flour mill in Ellicott City. He said without preamble: "I come straight from the mill when I heard the news. Can't hardly believe it." Usually a quiet man, Larry was more expressive about this than Dart had ever seen him. She relayed to him what she knew and he kept shaking his head in response.

Lou came up to them and said: "You want a National, Dart?" He referred to Baltimore's swill of choice, National Bohemian beer, affectionately known as Natty Bo, brewed in the city since 1886. Most of his patrons limited their drinking to National on tap.

"Yeah, thanks Lou."

As she waited for her drink, some people near them were having a loud discussion. The woman said to the man: ".....his widow's gone crazy. Said she damn near pulled her hair out when she heard the news. Started throwing things around saying she was going to find his killer if it's the last thing she ever does for Lester."

Dart and Larry looked at each other. The crowd was trading stories about Lester's death. The broadcasting of the Orioles home game on the television was even being ignored. Probably a lot of it had some basis in the truth but who knew what at this point.

Dart thought back to the previous evening. A small crowd had headed over to Ivanhoe's after the championship. Ralph from "Blaze 'O' Glory" had been there---sans the twins. Shirl and Larry from Dart's team had shown up. Wallie and Joe from "Colleen's Men" had also been there along with some of the guys from the mediocre teams. After the altercation between Lester and Bobby, half-hearted discussion had taken place about the points of the game.

"This is victory as it should be," Shirl had said. She ran her hand through her frizzy hair, dulled by too many home permanents.

Wallie, a beefy man with a black bouffant hairstyle a la Elvis, had leaned towards her and said: "You only got third, babe. Remember?"

She had grunted in reply.

"Now me and Joe here, we got the gold. Right, Joey?" He looked over at his teammate whose blood level had already risen in alcohol content. Content with gesturing to communicate, Joe held up his short, thick fingers making a victory sign to his lips with a slow, sucking sound.

21

Shirl had made a tossing motion with her hand. "Ah to hell with yous. Two more rounds and we woulda been champ-e-ons!" The league offered Shirl a welcome respite from the trails of her life which included a mentally retarded son and an absentee husband. She was heavily invested in her duckpin prowess.

She had rambled on: "Up fifteen pins in the ninth, working on the spare, cocky as all get out and then.....blast it!"

Larry had piped in: "Now, Shirl. Remember our bet...your mouth as sweet as pie for a whole month."

Shirl exhaled some cigarette smoke and then had changed the discussion. "I don't get it. I never heard Lester get out of hand like that. What was he up to?"

One of the other teams' players chimed in. "Shame for Bobby. He won't get individual champ. He must be burning bad."

Ralph had risen to Bobby's defense. "Lester set him up. He brought that female ringer in mid-season to replace that kid. That wasn't right, right there, but we all put up with it, didn't we?"

Shirl and Larry passed a look upon Ralph's pronouncement. Shirl had then knocked back the remainder of her beer and barked out "nother National" to Lou.

Dart had listened to all of it never thinking the next day's events would unfold as they did.

Chapter Five

Paging through the Baltimore Sun the following day, Dart found a small article that reported in blunt fashion the circumstances of Lester Holmes's death. She decided to clip it out just to have on hand in her files. As a researcher, she saved a lot of various odds and ends which was her excuse for being a pack rat.

She had a meeting set up for the day with a duckpin contact, Park Canby. Park had been the executive director of the National Duckpin Bowling Congress for as he put it "more years than I care to count." No longer the director, he still kept an active role in the Congress. He had contacted Dart to discuss the possibility of researching duckpin bowling and pulling a history pamphlet together for the Congress.

They had arranged to meet at the alley where Park used to bowl: Paradise Alley. She drove around the beltway that ringed the city of Baltimore and its environs until she reached the three o'clock position. Paradise Alley was on the smallish side, situated in a strip shopping center that dated from the 1940s. The stores in the strip were faded but it was possible to discern the streamlined modern style of another era.

Park Canby was waiting inside the alley by the soda counter. Park gave Dart a big smile as she walked towards him and then got up to shake hands.

"Park Canby, here. You must be Dart." He gestured towards a table where they could sit.

Park then said: "So what do you hear about Lester Holmes' death? That was something."

Dart replied: "Probably know about as much as you. Just what was in the paper today."

"A shame, a real shame," Park shook his head and then continued. "Well. What I am thinking about here is having you collect all the information you can from people that are getting a little long in the tooth, if you know what I mean. That way we won't lose valuable memories."

Dart went into her thoughts on how to best collect the data: mainly, through interviews and old newspaper clippings.

Park agreed with her thoughts and then said: "After you get everything together, we'll discuss how to print it up." He then went into how much money was available for the project and asked if that was agreeable to her.

She had already determined that this would be more of a labor of love than a moneymaker so she was fine with the arrangement.

"So, Park….how about if I get started today? You got a few minutes?"

He leaned back and said: "Sure, sure. Let's get started."

Dart began by asking about the heyday of duckpin at Paradise Alleys. It didn't take much to wind Park up. He sort of rolled off in helpful tangents all on his own. The man was a walking encyclopedia of duckpin lore.

"Here's the straight skinny on duckpin. It was invented around the turn of the century by two local boys. It chugged along until 1920 something when the Congress was formed." Dart knew all of this and considered Park to be accurate in reporting the facts thus far. She did not want to stem his flow but she really had another direction to discuss. She decided to wait it out until he wound down.

Park grew even more animated. "You see, Dart, once the Congress was formed that meant that the game became standardized----you know, regulation sizes and weights for the pins and the balls. And it led to having tournaments and such among the leagues."

Dart cut through. "Tell me about some of the people. The duckpin greats."

"Well, let's see. Aside from me, you mean?" Park gave a hearty laugh. "When I was coming out of the teen league and into adult, the one everybody spoke about in whispers was, of course, Al Garrity."

"Al Garrity?"

"Sure---you mean you never heard of Al?"

"No, I don't think so."

"You'd remember, that's for sure. Al was the top male bowler for twelve years straight with an overall average of 150 a game throughout the course of his bowling."

"What happened after twelve years?"

Park frowned. "It was a real sad thing. He was drinking---they said---and crashed his car one night."

"Why would 'they' say he was drinking if he hadn't been?"

Park looked around to see if anyone was within earshot. "It was a big scandal back in the day. A lot of us suspected foul play."

Dart made a mental note to check for newspaper articles about this. Park continued to chat about duckpin. When Dart brought up the rumored demise of duckpin, Park visibly bristled and changed the subject. He was obviously a romantic diehard and didn't want to entertain any such notions. His only comment had been: "You need to talk to Orv Haskins. He's got the angle. Give him a call."

Although the number of alleys had dwindled, the surviving alleys were owned and run by faithful duckpin fanatics. Orv Haskins owned and managed the Fontana Alley out in Randallstown. Dart had run into him from time to time in her league travels. She left the Paradise Alley with some good shots in her camera of Park and a glimpse into his corner of the duckpin world. She also had a good lead to follow with Orv Haskins.

She headed her car towards Ivanhoe's. It was practically on her way home if five traffic lights and several miles were considered practically.

Lou was bartending and greeted her with his usual, "What's up, Dart?"

Dart pulled up a barstool and breathed a heavy sigh. Lou poured her a draft of Natty Bo and placed it in front of her.

He said: "I'm sick of talking about who killed Lester. Tell me about something I don't know."

"How about duckpin bowling?"

"Sure. Why not?" He continued to wipe down the bar. It seemed to Dart that he was suspended in a perpetual wiping down the bar motion whenever she walked into Ivanhoe's.

"I got one for you that I heard this morning from a guy named Park Canby. Why is duckpin bowling called duckpin bowling?"

Lou shrugged.

"Because the shaved down pins looked like a flock of flying ducks when the ball struck. A Baltimore Sun sportswriter came up with that."

Lou gave a chuckle. "Never heard that one before."

Dart then asked him: "You ever hear of Al Garrity?" As Lou opened his mouth to respond, the door crashed open and Bobby Blaze stumbled into Ivanhoe's.

"Wha's up?" he asked looking blearily at some other point in the room.

Lou and Dart exchanged glances. Bobby did not have a reputation for showing up places intoxicated.

"Hey Bobby," Lou said breezily, "where you been?"

"I been round." He wiped a hand across his mouth and continued: "That damn detective keeps giving me the business."

"He's talked to you more than once?" Dart asked.

"Yeah, called me in to check out some more 'details', he said."

"Well, you got nothing to worry about, right, Bobby?" Lou added.

Bobby stared down at the bar and did not reply.

"Bobby?" Lou pressed him.

"Uh? Oh," shaking his head, Bobby slurred, "Never you mind about me, Lou. I'm squeekin' clean."

Dart looked down at her watch. "Geez, look at the time. I gotta run."

She made her exit leaving Lou to deal with a miserable Bobby Blaze.

Chapter Six

The next day, Dart called over to Citylanes to check in and Bobby answered. He caught her up with the latest which was that Lester's funeral was being delayed until the autopsy results were in. Also, some people in the league were pitching in for flowers and a money gift for Myra Holmes, Lester's widow. He asked if Dart would mind contributing---and delivering it.

Dart's stomach lurched. "You mean there's nobody else? Somebody who knows her better, maybe?"

Snippets of conversation from the other night at Ivanhoe's filtered into Dart's brain: "wild with grief", "gone crazy", "seeking vengeance."

Bobby answered: "Well, I guess Miss Ivy..."

Dart cut him short. "That's alright. Miss Ivy has enough on her plate. How about I pick the money up later this afternoon and deliver it then?"

They agreed on a time and ended the conversation.

That afternoon, the door to Citylanes was propped open. She walked up the stairs and called out hello. Bobby Blaze poked his head around the corner.

"Hey Dart," he greeted her. "I've got the money together right here." He handed her an envelope stuffed with bills. Then he added: "Some of the girls think you should get one of those fruit baskets. There's probably more than enough in there for that and just give her the rest."

"Got it." Dart hesitated and then said: "So...how is everything going?"

Bobby couldn't quite look her in the eye as he answered. She assumed he was embarrassed about his performance at Ivanhoe's the day before.

"Well....we've seen better days but we're getting through."

"Miss Ivy's not ready to come back yet?"

"To tell the truth, she is. Billy and I had to practically hog tie her to keep her at the house for a couple of days."

Dart grinned at the idea of Miss Ivy being hog tied.

"When are you going to open shop?"

"Tonight."

Dart looked surprised and Bobby followed with "We can't afford to stay closed. You know how tough it is to keep the regulars. If we turn them out....." his voice trailed off.

"I know, Bobby. Maybe I'll come out for a game tonight myself."

As Dart headed out, Bobby stopped her by asking: "Hey....you think that cop knows who did it?"

Dart turned back and said: "I don't know. I really don't."

Two blocks from the alley, a large rectangular building with a flat roof filled a city block and housed one of the city's markets, Cross Street Market. It supported vendors that sold everything from pigs' feet to fresh cut freesias. Upon entering the market, Dart inhaled the strange mixture of market smells. The regulars that Dart could always count on seeing milled about including the bearded lady pushing a pop up cart and the fishmonger who sported a beret. Dart stopped at stalls along the way taking in the colorful fruits, vegetables, baked goods, meats and fish. She finally ended up making a deal with a fruit vendor for a brightly cellophaned package of fruit.

She really craved romaine lettuce but it was not to be found. El Nino had put a screeching halt to all deliveries from California. California was the only source of romaine during Maryland's non-growing season. Her cravings for romaine would not be satisfied for awhile. Looking at her watch, she realized she had not eaten lunch yet and wandered over to the sausage stand.

As she walked up, Detective Marino was just taking a big bite out of a sausage wrapped in a bun. She noted how he wore his hair longish almost in a ducktail style.

"Fancy meeting you here," she commented to him.

He finished chewing and said: "Hello Miz Hastings. What's going on?"

"Nothing much. Just grabbing a late lunch....so why aren't you at the Italian sub shop instead? With a name like Marino...."

"Because bratwurst is a treat and my mother is German."

The lady manning the stand snapped her gum and said to Dart: "Can I help you?"

Dart ordered a sausage with chili and onions on top. Marino continued to stand around and chew.

He then said between bites: "Anything going on at the alley lately?"

"Yeah, they're opening back up tonight." Dart flashed back on Bobby's behavior at the bar. Was that something she should share? She didn't see why she had to but....

Marino could see dilemma on Dart's face. His eyes narrowed. "You got something to tell me?"

"Well, actually, yeah. Our mothers play canasta together."

Dart saw confusion pass over his face and continued: "They're in the same group. I had dinner with my mom the other night."

"Wait a minute. Your mom isn't the Mrs. Hastings that makes those great brownies is she?"

"The very same," Dart replied.

"Well, how about that? They say Baltimore is a town of two separations." He leaned back on the counter. "So....you hear anything from other people in the league that I should know about?"

"What am I? A spy or something?"

Marino chuckled and then said: "It's pretty straightforward. Do you have any more thoughts on the case? Any ideas?" He followed with: "You seem to know all the players involved and you might have some insider's insight to the whole thing."

Dart hesitated. "No, there's really nothing other than the scene between Bobby and Lester which you already know about."

Marino didn't miss the hesitation and pursued it. "I'm talking anything here. Somebody looking at somebody else crossed eyed. That kind of thing."

Dart said: "I got nothing for you. So....do you have any suspects yet?"

He winked at her and said: "Police biz."

She felt irritation. "Look, Marino. You ask me for information but how can I help if I don't know what direction you are going in?"

Marino smiled broadly and suddenly appeared more human. "Two way street, uh?"

Dart sniped: "It's a deal if you keep your end of it."

He put his hands up in mock defense. "Okay, okay. At this point, anything is fair game. Just keep your ears and eyes open."

After leaving the market and the irritating Marino behind, Dart headed out into the wilds of the county and ended up at a run-down rancher with a dried out front yard. Myra Holmes answered her door, and Dart offered her the fruit basket. Myra, a woman with almost alabaster skin and jet black hair, was still in her housecoat. She invited Dart in. As Dart stepped inside, a gray French poodle snapped at her ankles.

"Oh scat, Rascal. Just get outta here."

The dog seemed almost to sniff in offense as he left the room. Myra sank into a ratty sofa and held a handkerchief close to her face. Dart attempted to express the league's condolences but was quickly cut off.

"He was such a good man. People just didn't realize that."

Dart said: "Well....I'm sure...."

"He struggled his whole life," then she added in between sobs, "Did you ever hear him talk about his military career?"

It had been Dart's understanding that Lester had only served two years as an enlisted man but she played along. "Yes, I...."

Myra cut off Dart again and began to go into more memories of Lester.

Finally, Dart got a word in edgewise and asked if Myra had any ideas on who could have done such a horrible thing to her husband.

That question was received with a fresh burst of sobs and then Myra said: "Can you believe they haven't figured it out yet?" Dart noted how Myra had avoided answering the question. She then asked Myra about the funeral arrangements.

Myra said: "It will be held at St. Leo's, of course. But they won't let me know when I can...when his body will be ready. You'll be there?"

Dart was taken aback and then said: "Of course, of course." A bit later, she managed to say her goodbyes tripping over the poodle as she left.

Chapter Seven

The scene at Myra's took a toll on Dart and she wound up at Ivanhoe's. Opening the door, she left the sunshine for the coolness of the air conditioning and the dark red tones. She asked Lou for a draft and reflected back on her conversation with Marino. The murder of Lester Holmes had occurred several days earlier, and Marino didn't appear to have a clue. Especially if he was relying on her for input. Although Dart did recognize the fact that she might have more of an insider's track by hanging around the neighborhood, namely Ivanhoe's and the alley.

There was only a smattering of folks at the bar. Shirl was the only one there from the league. A couple of guys were running the pool table and a large woman with a long haired ponytail sat on the stool in front of the only video poker machine. At one point, the woman had leaped off the stool and shouted "Hooah!" as the machine rang up a series of points. But, for the most part, she seemed to put an endless supply of quarters into it.

Dart leaned over to Shirl and commented: "Geez, you'd think she could find a better way to spend her money."

Shirl looked at Dart incredulously. "Honey, she's betting to win."

"What are you talking about? That's illegal. Like the machine says: 'For Amusement/Entertainment Only'."

"Oh boy, were you born yesterday Dart or what? Every machine in this city pays out."

Dart was dumbfounded. She prided herself on being an insider. How had she missed out on knowing this bit of local gaming? It brought to mind the old saw: Don't overlook the obvious.

"Look," Shirl said. "Look right now." The woman was off the stool and walking over to Lou. He peered around the machine which registered five hundred and some points. With that, he reached into a box, pulled out some bills and handed it over to the woman.

Shirl blew some smoke curls. "There's a racket everywhere you go, Dart. You should know that by now."

Shirl gestured for Lou to pour her another and toyed with her empty draft glass. She had already been there awhile judging from the slight slur to her words. Shirl then said: "Take our friendly neighborhood league, for 'xample."

Dart's ears perked up. "What about it?"

"Ah never mind. I shouldn't be talking 'bout nothing."

Dart coaxed: "Come on Shirl. You brought it up. Anything said at Ivanhoe's is in the vault. I know that."

Shirl gave a guffaw. Then she looked around her before saying: "Miss Ivy and Billy ain't as innocent with those books as it seems."

"Miss Ivy??"

"Well...a bunch of us had some other money riding on the league. Not everybody. Just a few."

"Like who?"

"Well, " Shirl ran a hand through her hair, "let's see----me, Ralph, Billy and Bobby, Carmen. And Lester. I guess that was all."

"What kind of money are we talking about?"

"Enough to make it worth betting on."

Dart mused aloud. "You don't think....could that be the motive for Lester's death?"

Shirl squirmed. "Aww. Come on now Dart. Don't talk like that."

Dart protested. "Shirl, I'm just trying to make sense of this thing. What do you think?"

Shirl looked the other way. Then she said: "I gotta be going home."

"Shirl!" Dart called after Shirl as she stumbled off the barstool and went outside into the harsh light. She left a half finished draft at her spot at the bar.

Dart had stayed at Ivanhoe's a bit too long and walked off some of the beer by heading over to Citylanes. It was early but she intended on grabbing a hot dog for dinner before rolling some balls. When she got near the alley, she was astounded to see a line outside of the building. "What the hell," she thought to herself. She skirted past the crowd and saw Billy seated at a table in the front. He waved her by. The scene inside the alley was chaos. Some were bowling but the majority of people were standing around talking. Snatches of conversation included: "I heard his wife is crazy as a mudhen----I bet she did it!" and "Lester was always in trouble coming up in the neighborhood" and "Did you see that blowhard, Bobby?" Lane seven was conspicuously not in use by any of the bowlers.

Dart edged over to Wallie in the crowd and asked what was happening. Wallie leaned towards her and said: "That owner came back from the Bahamas when he heard about Lester. They're saying he's going to make an announcement 'bout something."

Before Dart had a chance to ask Wallie for more details, Bobby Blaze stepped up in the front and center and clapped his hands. Using a microphone, he announced: "Hey, hey everybody. Great turnout! We got a couple of people here tonight that have a few words to say. First off, let me introduce the owner of Citylanes, Cal Lombard."

A nattily dressed man anywhere from age fifty to age seventy-five took the mike that Bobby handed to him. His astoundingly blue eyes focused on the group of people in the room. He wore a three piece tweed suit of good quality. He still had a full head of hair which was carefully parted on the side and slicked back. His skin was deeply tanned reflecting his time in the islands. The piece de la resistance of his ensemble was a silk tie, circa 1940s, that had been airbrushed with a design of duckpins laying haphazardly on a mauve background. The tie was spectacular.

Cal spoke carefully into the mike: "Thanks, Bobby. I'd like to thank everyone for their continued support through these trying times at the alley." Cal's voice carried a hint of a posh accent maybe from the upper crust sections of town such as Guilford or Homewood.

He continued: "Without further ado, I hand these proceedings over to Dennys Smith, the Executive Director of the National Duckpin Bowling Congress!"

There were a few snickers in the crowd indicating the mixed feelings that players felt for the Congress and its role in leagues and alleys. Dart knew that historically the Congress had provided legitimacy to duckpin bowling. Now, however, alley owners and league players did not feel they were getting much "bang for the buck" when they paid Congress dues. Unfortunately, if the Congress folded, the truth of the matter was that standards would unravel and the sport would suffer even more.

Dennys Smith was a slender man with a feminine air about him. He was someone that Dart felt she had met in a past life whenever she was in his presence. Dennys took over the proceedings and said with confidence: "Hello, folks. I second Mr. Lombard's appreciation for supporting the alley tonight because, in doing so, you also support the sport in general. We're here tonight to offer a reward for information leading to the apprehension of Lester Holme's murderer." There was an immediate buzz in the crowd. "That's right. The Congress has pulled some funds together and we're offering $2500 to the person or persons who can help us out on this. Needless to say, we're very unhappy about all that has happened but hope to get justice for Lester sooner rather than later. Don't forget folks: This is duckpin country!" He handed the mike back to Bobby but then snatched it back and said: "And don't forget to sign up for the next league!"

Bobby then told everyone to enjoy themselves and that sodas were on the house until 10:00 p.m.

Dart wandered over to where Cal Lombard and Dennys Smith were in a tete a tete. She offered a hand to Dennys: "Hi Dennys. I'm Dart Hastings. I've met you at several Congress banquets. You guys put on a good spread."

Dennis gave an unctuous smile and replied: "Of course, Dart. Thanks for the compliment. You know Cal Lombard?"

Dart said: "Actually, we have never met. Hello, Mr. Lombard. I play on the Citylanes league."

Cal nodded his head in a pleased to meet you gesture.

"That's a fantastic vintage tie you have on tonight," Dart said pointing to Cal's chest.

"Oh, this old thing. I got this years ago when I was playing in the Hamilton Alley league. It was great fun."

"So what prompted this reward money?" Dart asked the men.

Cal and Dennys looked at each other and then both leaned towards Dart in a confidential manner.

Cal said: "Dart, here's how we see it. Look at the crowd that came out tonight. The notoriety of Lester's death is ironically bringing in business. This reward will fuel that fire and keep this alley afloat."

Dennys chimed in: "You may find this callous but you know how duckpin is dying on the vine. We need to maximize every opportunity....and Lester's murderer still needs to be caught. It's a crime in and of itself they haven't figured this out yet."

Dart felt uneasy. She didn't approve of their tactics...but duckpin was losing ground to tenpin bowling every year. And who knew how much longer the little duckpin alleys could keep chugging along. Citylanes, like all the others, operated on a shoestring budget at best. There were salaries, rents and electricity to pay at a minimum.

Both men were looking at her for a response. She asked them: "What happens when someone provides the information? Won't it all just go back to how it was?"

Dennys shrugged and said: "These things are hard to predict. We'll keep the hoopla going for as long as we can. Let's face it. Duckpin is on borrowed time anyway."

Cal nodded sadly. "My alley is in good standing. Miss Ivy does a wonderful job in keeping us in the black. But there will soon come a day....."

Dart left the alley in a deflated mood. She thought about the reward money. What if she figured out who did this? She knew all the players. It had to be an inside job as Marino had hinted and who better to figure it out than someone like her? In a weird way, it might help her with Park Canby's research project.

It wasn't about the money---although it would be nice to take a trip down to the ocean. Maybe get some of that tan that Cal Lombard sported. It was more about the challenge----kind of like a crossword puzzle.

Back at her apartment, Dart sat at her desk and fiddled with two small glass paperweights; one with a pressed dead butterfly and the other with marbleized glass. She then picked up Marino's business card and stared at it. It included a mobile number. Thoughtfully, she picked up the phone and dialed the number.

He answered: "Marino, here."

"Hey, it's Dart Hastings."

"Whatta you got for me?"

Marino didn't waste any words. Dart replied: "Thought you might want to know that Cal Lombard is back in town. Remember---he's the owner of Citylanes? Anyway, he and the Duckpin Congress announced a $2500 reward tonight at the alley for information leading to the killer's arrest."

Marino gave a low whistle. "Don't trust the boys in blue, eh?"

"Something like that, I guess. So....I've been doing some thinking."

"Uh-oh. Is it amateur detective hour?" he said laughing.

"Hear me out. If you can feed me some information, I know I can help figure this out. Think about it. I know a lot of people in the league and the neighborhood."

"Yeah, I know. That's why I said keep your eyes and ears open."

"Right. But I need more to work with."

"Alright, Hastings. I'll bite. What do you want to know?"

"How did Lester die?"

Marino was silent and Dart figured the conversation was over. Then he said: "He was struck with a blunt instrument between 11:00 p.m. and 12:00 a.m. Left somewhere to bleed to death until an estimated 3:00 a.m. Brought to the alley and hoisted up into Lane seven anywhere from 3:00 a.m. to when Miss Ivy and Billy claim to have shown up at 9:30 a.m."

"Claim to have shown up?"

"You want the facts, right? Anything else I can help you with?"

Dart answered: "That will do for now."

After hanging up with Marino, Dart pulled out a fresh legal pad and drew a diagram. Her research was taking a new spin.

On the other side of the beltway, Marino hung up and shook his head. It was probably not a good thing to let Dart Hastings get involved. He would have to make sure she didn't get into trouble.

He decided to take a trip downtown. Parking a couple of blocks from Citylanes, he got out of his car. He walked on the other side of the street and looked across at Citylanes. Apparently, the earlier hulabuloo had died down but there were still some lights on from within, possibly security lighting. Marino stood and studied the building in front of him. The bowling alley took up the second and third floors of the building. The wide expanse of commercial storefront windows exposed the duckpin machinery within. In the cloak of night, however, it would be possible to work on the other side of the machinery without anyone from the street observing. Even when lit up, it was only backlit from the lights deeper in the alley.

The question was how did they string his body up there? Marino had thoroughly studied the mechanism of the setting machine, and it was reliant on a balanced weight system. Since Lester's body added to the weight of the ten duckpins combined, it was necessary for the killer to add weights to the other side in order for the front side to be balanced. Bringing Lester and the duckpins down into place involved an electrical signal pressed from the front of the lane. When Miss Ivy and Billy had pressed the button, down came Lester draped over the group of duckpins.

Seeing the lit up machinery from the street with its innards revealed, Marino felt anger. The pressure was on for him to figure this out. Now some hot shot businessman had to turn it up higher and offer a reward. Marino knew he must be overlooking something obvious. But what?

Chapter Eight

Lester's funeral was a grim affair. His widow had insisted, to the chagrin of the funeral home director, that his open coffin contain a bowling ball and a duckpin. Myra had donned a long black veil and sobbed loudly throughout the service. It seemed to Dart that she wanted to drive the point home that she was indeed the grieving widow. Looking around during the service, Dart noted the attendance of several league members including his teammates from Colleen's Men, Wallie and Joe.

Afterwards, as the hearse pulled away to the cemetery, a small number of people hung around the church steps unsure of themselves. Dart approached Wallie and Joe who stood together smoking cigarettes. They said hello and Joe offered her a smoke. She declined the offer.

No one talked until Joe broke the silence and said: "It was a nice ceremony. Lester woulda liked it."

Dart said: "You guys are going to miss him I bet. He was a great bowler. What did he average, 130?"

"Yeah, that's right," Wallie replied.

Joe said: "Maybe he was too good of a bowler."

"What do you mean?" Dart asked as Wallie threw Joe a sneer.

"Nothing, nothing...it's just that....well, who could have done this other than Bobby? You tell me. Bobby could never stand losing even when we was kids coming up in the teen leagues. He couldn't stand it that Lester was good. And that's the God's honest truth."

After Joe finished, Wallie added: "We don't know nothing for sure but it seems pretty tell-tale."

Dart was at a loss of what to say. "Have you talked to the cops about what you think?"

"Hell no. I ain't talking to no cop about nothing." Wallie backed down the steps and said to Joe: "Let's get outta here."

Stepping away, Joe looked at Dart and said: "See you around."

Dart shook her head and stepped off towards her car. She had an appointment with Orv Haskins, the owner of Fontana Alley. He had suggested she stop by when the alley had customers. She didn't understand what he meant by that but had gone along with the plan.

The Fontana was located on a major artery heading west out of Baltimore City. A "miracle mile" commercial strip had filled in since the alley had been built. The Fontana was currently squeezed in between a Dairy Queen and an auto glass shop. The alley was housed in a large warehouse covered with tin. A neon sign dating from the 1960s proclaimed it to be the Fontana. It had still managed to retain its big gravel parking lot which was a sizable chunk of real estate worth a mint for that plot alone. The parking lot had a few cars parked here and there. It was a wonder that Orv had not sold out yet.

Dart walked into the alley and looked around for Orv over the sweeping lanes of the Fontana which spread the width of the warehouse building. Orv, heavy set with a thick, silver mane, was talking with a group of bowlers on one of the lanes. Dart recognized him from social occasions put on by the Congress. On sighting him, she remembered earlier impressions of him being a happy-go-lucky type seemingly unphased by the vagaries of time and life.

He wrapped up his conversation and came over to Dart, grabbing her hand and giving it a good hearty shake. They went back into his office. Orv launched into a one-sided conversation about the business. "So what I got going on here is a deal where I open up for groups who have made appointments. That way, I cut way down on my overhead, deal with some real loyal customers and still keep the thing going. See what I mean?"

Dart thought it through. Opening the alley just occasionally surely couldn't bring in an income and she commented as such. Orv brushed her comment aside. "Oh, now. I do fine. Really, I think it's where we're going with duckpin. Got to go. This way the customers can keep things going."

Dart had trouble following the financial logic but didn't say anything further. If he was happy with it, so be it. He continued to comment that it allowed him plenty of time to catch up with paperwork as he swept a hand across a littered desk. Dart noticed some racing forms peeking out from under and thought to herself: "Paperwork. So that's what it's called these days...."

She said out loud: "Well, Orv. I just want to ask you some questions about the old days. You know, when duckpin experienced its hey day and you started up the alley."

"Sure---fire away."

Dart took out her notebook. "So what was the highpoint of Fontana's?"

Orv scratched his head giving it some thought. "Hhmm...I guess that would be when we sent one of our own to the Congress championships back in '77."

"Who was that?"

Orv shifted in his chair and looked at Dart. Finally, he said: "Lester Holmes."

Dart gulped and said: "I didn't know Lester had ever bowled out here. I thought he was born and bred in South Baltimore."

"No, no....not everybody remembers them days...but having Lester bowl here helped put the Fontana in good standing."

"I guess his death must have come as a shock to you."

Orv's face was grim. "Me and everybody else, right?"

Dart looked down at her notebook trying to get the interview back on track. As she searched for her next question, a bowler stomped into Orv's office.

"Hey, Orv. We got a jam in Lane Five. You wanna get it fixed for us?"

Orv said: "Just hold your horses. I'll be right there." He rose from his chair and smiled at Dart apologetically. "I don't want to hold you up but I can't say for sure how long this might take. How about you come back again? Could you do that?"

Dart groaned inwardly but told Orv she would do just that. As an afterthought, she asked: "Okay if I stroll around and take some photos?"

Orv waved a hand for her to help herself.

Dart got up and stretched. Orv's office walls were covered with framed photographs. Her eyes stopped on one which depicted Orv and Lester arm in arm. Lester's free arm held up a trophy. Dart barely recognized him as the Lester she had known. His face was young and unlined; no signs of the hard life that had come later. Both men had ebullient expressions on their faces. The bottom of the frame had a plated caption: 1968 National Duckpin Congress Championships, Fontana Alley.

Shaking her head, Dart collected her things and walked out into the main area. Once she pulled out the camera and checked its settings, she looked around for photo opportunities. There were some old posters announcing Congress games that showed some splashes of color against the otherwise beige walls.

After shooting some close-ups, she noticed that in the lanes above each scoring table hung single bulb light fixtures like those seen over poker tables. Using her wide angle lens, she captured them in a line.

Finished with her "artsy" shots, she scoped out the rest of the space. The crowd was sparse. There was an elderly couple dressed alike in light colored polyester in one of the lanes. Dart approached them and asked if she could take some photographs, explaining her purpose. The lady looked at her suspiciously while the man said: "Sure, hon." Dart hung back until she got her perfect shot. The lady scored a strike and then turned back to her husband with a smile that transformed her homely face.

After some more general photos, Dart realized that Orv wasn't going to be free anytime soon and resigned herself to coming back for another visit.

Chapter Nine

There was only one place in the city of Baltimore that spelled research. The Enoch Pratt Central Library was a bastion of the city's civic affairs. Taking up a central location in the Mount Vernon neighborhood, the Pratt was a tribute to the architectural glory days when details and features were artistically created and maintained with care. Dart always marveled at the heavy brass fixtures on the main doors as she headed into the library. Once inside the main room, the room's height extended about thirty-five feet. The top floor was surrounded by an ornate balcony. The space spoke volumes of an earlier era of civic buildings.

Dart headed to a second floor room that housed microfilm of newspapers and magazines. Once there, she stationed herself at a table and began to delve into the indexes. First on her list was to pinpoint an obituary for Al Garrity. Two hours later, she had not hit pay dirt and was discouraged. Not only discouraged but irritated by several patrons in the room who were mainly there to share burps, flatulence and the like and take up space.

She decided to divert the course of her research and look through old duckpin bowling news. From 1943 to 1979, there had been a local periodical called *Duckpin Details* that was produced by the Congress and a small publishing house on a quarterly basis. The Pratt had almost all the back copies available in folders and microfilm to Dart's delight.

She randomly picked through some 1950s issues and then moved into the 1960s. The news of the leagues and the alleys from those time frames were priceless. Tidbits about players and techniques were presented in a colloquial Baltimoresque manner. She laughed outloud at a photograph of the Congress champion from 1963. With his ducktail hairdo, horn-rimmed glasses and loud striped shirt, the guy looked like a regular lady killer.

Finally, in some of the 60s issues, Miss Ivy began to appear as the female champion. A full photo shoot was done at the end of each year showing the male and female champions and other award receivers. In 1968, Miss Ivy was paired up with Al Garrity in a photograph, both smiling widely into the camera lens. This was the same photo she had found under Miss Ivy's desk. So the mystery man was Al Garrity, the famed bowler that Park Canby had brought to her attention.

It was a 1969 issue that made Dart gasp. It presented a memorial to one Al Garrity complete with photographs of his funeral. In one photograph, his family was assembled and solemn-faced. Eerily in the background, Dart recognized Miss Ivy looking towards the camera with an odd grin on her face.

Pouring through the story of Garrity's life, Dart became wrapped up in the details of him as a well-liked family man, a pillar of the community and an all-around great guy by all accounts. She couldn't figure it out. What was the connection between him and Miss Ivy? Maybe the answer was still with the Garrity family.

It was then that Dart discovered a folder stuck inside one of the issues. Inside, there were some newsclippings and photographs all pertaining to one Albert "Al" Garrity, the male duckpin champion for a period of twelve years. Dart opened them up and began to read. The clippings ran from year to year and included the newspaper write-ups on his championships.

One clipping was an interview with Al and his family and included photos of him posing on a nice, big lawn with five children and a June Cleaver style wife. It discussed the family's weekly church attendance at St. Alphonsus, their bowling involvement and other family oriented events. Al was a sharp looking fellow with a full head of hair and long eye lashes. He held a job as a civil engineer with the Army Corps of Engineers in downtown Baltimore. One 8 x 10 glossy in a separate manila envelope showed a studio portrait of the man with a devilish grin on his face sporting a wonderful duckpin bowling tie.

Finally, Dart read about the untimely death of Al Garrity due to a car accident on Taylor Avenue. According to the news article, he had been driving while intoxicated and lost control of the car. Police investigators, it was noted, had some reservations about the circumstances of the accident but there were no further articles.

Dart, exhausted, trudged up the stairs to her apartment. After a lackluster greeting to the meowing Marvin, she headed into the kitchen. Hunger was foremost on her mind and she pulled out a can of chunky chicken noodle soup and dumped it in a saucepan.

Fifteen minutes later, Dart washed down her last spoonful of soup. She sat back and gave a delicate belch. Surveying around her, she made a mental list: Marvin needed to be fed, the kitchen needed cleaning, and---her eye caught the blink of the message machine. One beep meant one message. Great she thought to herself. She was in no mood to talk to any clients.

Jamming the button, she listened to the message. It was from Miss Ivy. Her voice, as chirpy as ever, piped through: "Hi Dart. Miss Ivy here. I just wanted to remind you the sign up deadline for the summer league is this week. You want to be sure to get your name and money into me, hon."

Dart stared at the machine, puzzled. What was she missing? Miss Ivy had found a dead body less than a week ago but yet she was composed enough to call people for the summer league? Dart thought to herself: "Listening to her speak, you'd never know a tragedy had taken place in her alley."

Dart's mind wandered to the issue at hand. Did she want to sign up for the summer league? She had originally planned on it. It was only a ten week league and she would stay in practice for the fall. Of course, it did mean squeezing twelve dollars a week out of her already meager budget. But it had always been a good time.

She wasn't quite sure she wanted to sign up with Lester's death hanging over everything like a shroud. Maybe some could ignore it but she didn't think she could without replaying the scenario right in front of lane seven. She would let Miss Ivy know that she was taking the summer off.

Burnt out on her research endeavors, Dart headed over to the south side of the city and got to Ivanhoe's. She took a sip of her ice cold draft and felt some tension release from her shoulder blades. She massaged her temples with one hand.

Lou wiped a dishrag across the bar, his huge meaty arms making short work of the job, and came down to where she was seated on a stool. "Tough day in the trenches?" he asked.

"Yeah, you could say that."

"You mean the life of the self-employed ain't all it's cracked up to be?"

Dart gave a grunt and replied: "Not when you're 34 and holding."

She sighed deeply and wished for her cigarette smoking days. Looking around, she realized it was just her and Lou. A slow night she guessed.

"Where is everybody, Lou?"

"You've started kind of early tonight, Dart."

"So…you hear anything about Lester? I've been out of the loop today."

"Achh…you're asking the wrong guy."

"How's that?"

"I know too much."

Dart sat up a little straighter. "Then why don't you go for that reward money?"

"I'm not making no waves. I got enough to worry about."

"Then why don't you tell me so I can go for that reward money?"

Lou took a drag from a cigarette in a tray behind the bar and looked at her though squinted eyes. After blowing the smoke out, he said, "Well…."

The door to Ivanhoe's swung open at that second and a couple of guys walked towards the bar. Lou directed his words to them instead: "What'll it be fellows?"

Dart got up to use the ladies room. While doing her business, she stared at the graffiti filled wall and picked up on a line that read: "I keep drowning my troubles but the g-damn things keep learning how to swim." When she returned to the bar, Lou was free again. She looked at him and said: "Well?"

He leaned forward and said: "Three words, okay? That's all I got for you. Hi-Ho-Pimlico."

He stood back and walked down to the other customers at the end of the bar.

Dart considered Lou's words. So maybe Lester had like to gamble at the track. So Lester was also involved in the betting on the league. Lester and money. Money had gotten him into trouble.

Dart decided that the next day might be the perfect choice for a day at the races.

Chapter Ten

While Dart sat in Ivanhoe's drinking some cold ones, Marino was already down at the track. He had gotten a lead on a guy named Tom from Lester's widow, Myra. Myra had claimed that this guy would repeatedly call the house leaving messages for Lester and referred to himself as a friend from the track. Marino had asked Myra what Lester's preference had been out of the two tracks in the area and she had said Pimlico whenever the horses were running there.

The late afternoon was overcast and the crowd was sparse as typical of a weekday at the track. Marino grabbed a coke and then placed a bet for the next race: $2.00 for "Midnight Madness" to place. He wandered around and finally set his sights on a group of men hanging around one of the monitors. They had the look of well-seasoned track regulars.

"You know who looks good for the next race," he directed the question to the group in general.

"Yeah," a snaggle toothed man spoke up, "We're looking at 'Tsar's Favorite'."

The men continued their discussion. Marino caught the general drift which was something about the photo finish from the last race---no one seemed to be too pleased by the outcome. The race began and Marino stood with the other men watching it on the monitor.

As the horses pulled near the finish, some began yelling. When it was over, Marino looked down at his ticket. He had actually won a couple bucks. The man next to him said: "Win something?"

"Yeah, I did. Didn't expect it. I'm just killing time 'til I meet my buddy."

The man nodded in response.

Marino continued. "Hey---you wouldn't know him by any chance would you? Name's Lester Holmes."

The man shook his head and then said to the group: "Anybody know a Lester Holmes."

Another man spoke up: "You didn't hear? He kicked off, buddy."

"You gotta be kidding me. He owed me some money." Marino lied glibly.

One of the men sniffed. "You and everybody else too."

Another piped in. "That's right. Take a number." They all chuckled.

"You know anybody that's collected on him?"

"Well if anybody has it would be Tom."

"He around today?"

"Sure. Where else would he be? He's right over there." He pointed in the direction of a skinny guy in a garish polyester jacket with a matching cap. The man was busy studying the racing forms.

Marino made his way over and said, "Tom!"

Tom looked up with one eye and replied, "Who wants to know?"

"Name's Al. I was looking for a guy named Lester. He owed me some money."

"Owed is the word. You don't have a shot now."

"Yeah, I just figured that out. It hurts. What did he owe you for?"

"Oh, about 6 months of betting debt."

Marino let out a low whistle. "That's a lot of bets. What---about $10,000 or so?"

He looked at Marino and said: "Don't worry about it, pal."

Marino was silent and then continued, "No chance of getting it either."

"That's right."

"Any idea who offed him?"

"A lot of people around here didn't like the way Lester was doing business...."

Marino looked at him sharply and Tom sensed the change. "Hey---the guy liked to bet on the ponies too much. That my problem?"

"You want to give me the name of some of those people that didn't like Lester?"

"Now why would I do that?"

Marino flashed his badge.

"Alright, alright. I shoulda figured you for a cop. There's a guy out in the bleachers. Big guy, I mean real big guy. Bald with dark glasses. He works for the main man." As Marino walked off, Tom yelled "And drop me out of this."

Marino tracked down the "real big guy" and took some photos of him with one of the nifty mini digital cameras that the department doled out to a chosen few.

He got the images printed up in record time at a one hour photo place and then made his way back to the department. Once there, he collapsed at his desk and called one of the other detectives over.
"Tony, what do you make of this?" he asked.

Tony Rodriguez was one of the top guys handling undercover operations to pin down organized crime in Baltimore. A diamond in the rough, he played the street scene well and somehow kept his neck above water.

"Whadda you got there?" He picked up the photographs and sifted through them. Without missing a beat, he said: "That's Bunny, he runs things around the tracks."

"Runs things" implied that Bunny controlled the money loaning business end of things at the races.

"That's what I figured. You got anything on him so I can haul him in for questioning?"

"Sure, sure. I'll think of something." Tony replied.

Chapter Eleven

The next day Dart got up to the track at Pimlico by the early afternoon. She bought a beer and a racing program and took a seat. After perusing the program, she placed her bets at the racing window. Tickets in hand, she walked out towards the bleachers. On the way she passed a janitor cleaning up a spill on the concrete floor. Youngish and fresh faced, he seemed to be a safe target. "Hey, can you tell me what the best seating area is?"

He directed her to an upstairs area and explained how to get there. Dart thanked him and then said "Oh, I almost forgot I'm looking for a friend. Guy named Lester. About yay tall." She gestured.

"I'm pretty new here. I don't know many people. You might check with Ernie. He knows everybody. He's usually upstairs, has a goatee."

Dart made her way upstairs on the lookout for goateed men. On the way, she took in the sights. The track was always a people watcher's event extraordinaire. The ultimate contrast between the haves and have nots. Where else did you find beautiful show girl types with long blonde tresses, lacquered on dresses and stiletto heels on the arms of the millionaire horse owners mixing in the same space with octogenarians spending their last buck on a bet?

Once upstairs, Dart stood behind a man with dread locks at the bar waiting for a liquor drink. How could she find this guy Ernie?

Ask and you shall receive. A skinny man in a disheveled grey uniform that sported the nametag, "Ernie", and a wispy goatee, walked by her in line.

Dart hopped out of line and followed him. He stopped and leaned against a corner, pulling out a pack of cigarettes. "Damn", she thought to herself. "I can't use that as an excuse."

Instead, she put wishful thinking aside and asked him where the ladies room was. He began to tell her in great detail. She was quickly able to strike up a conversation with him. It was evident that he was an unofficial ambassador of sorts for the track. Once Dart felt that the entree had been made, she asked him about Lester.

"Weird guy. He used to come here oh every other afternoon or so. Got off from his job early in afternoons. Had time on his hands. He was a quiet sort but he sometimes talked to me." He gave a big grin. "I can usually get anybody to talk."

Ernie continued: "One thing real funny about the guy...he was a big duckpin bowler see? So his good luck thing was to always bet the amount of money equal to his bowling score for that week. Said that was his lucky system. Judging from what I've seen, it didn't work out all that well."

"Was he in debt?"

"Is the Pope Catholic?"

"That much uh?"

"Shi-i-t, but he was in deep. Used to pay visits to the Easter Bunny if you know what I mean."

"No actually I don't know what you mean.."

"Bunny...he's the resident loan shark around here. Lends them money and then breaks their arms if they don't pay up with interest. I'm probably talking out of school now. I better shut up."

Dart put up her hand to stop him from walking off. "Just one more question....what do you think happened to him?"

Ernie looked thoughtful and then said. "I do know the guy had some fancy big dreams. Claimed he had something on somebody that was going to keep him flush for awhile."

"Any idea what it was?

"Naahh. He talked double talk a lot. He only said something about money might be growing on vines. Don't know what the hell that meant."

"One more thing. Where's the Easter Bunny?"

Ernie put his hands over his eyes from the glare and stared out into the crowd. "He's right there." He pointed out a large bald man with big ears. "But hey, be careful with him, you hear?"

Dart thought about her next move while keeping her eyes pinned on Bunny. Almost a comical figure, he sat still watching the race. Just as Dart was getting up to venture down to Bunny's territory, she saw a figure sit down right next to Bunny. She strained her eyes and couldn't believe it. She recognized that natty attire and the dapper hairdo. Cal Lombard. Why was he talking to Bunny?

She got to her feet quick and rushed through the crowd searching for Ernie. Finding him on the other side of the building, she grabbed his sleeve and said before he had time to balk "Who's that standing next to Bunny?"

Ernie sighed deep and said: "Look, lady. This is getting old." Persuaded by her imploring eyes, he looked down to Bunny's corner and said: "That's Crazy Cal." She gave him the look again. "Bunny's main man."

Dart sprinted for a bank of phones. Once Marino was on the line, she asked: "Ever hear of an Easter Bunny that breaks arms?"

"Where the hell are you?" Marino asked.

When she said Pimlico, he told her to leave immediately, not talk to anyone on the way out and meet him at 6:00 at Frazier's Tap Room in Hampden.

Wallking out of the grandstand area, a snaggle toothed man in a faded checkered shirt leaned closely in towards her and said into her ear with emphasis: "God, you're beautiful." She kept walking straight on, the smell of his stale alcohol breath in her nose.

Chapter Twelve

Dart knew the place. It had been a favorite of her father's back in the day when he courted clients and customers. In the lower level of a rowhouse in a small city neighborhood, the place had a character all of its own. It served up standard American fare with a focus on meat and potatoes. That night's special was sour beef and dumplings. The interior consisted of a bar back and several tables decorated with old photographs of the neighborhood.

When Dart walked in, Marino was already seated perusing the menu. As she walked towards the table, he looked up and stared pointedly at her. It was not a nice stare she noted.

Getting to the table, she held out her hands. "What? Do they need slapping?"

"They don't. Something else maybe does."

Hhhmm, Dart thought. He's getting into some grey area. Out loud she said, "Hey, I'm on top of things. Helping you out remember?"

"Tracking down crime rings wasn't what I had in mind. Now why don't you give me a run-down on what happened?"

Dart recounted her day at the track in between ordering a highball and then dinner.

Marino stopped her often and questioned different points of the account. She finally got to the part where she had watched Bunny. Taking a big gulp of her drink and smacking her lips afterwards, she then said, "And just when I got up from my seat to go downstairs Bunny's got company."

Marino lifted an eyebrow.

Dart answered without being asked: "Cal Lombard." Marino's eyebrow lifted even higher. "I then track down Ernie who tells me Cal is Bunny's main man!" Triumphant she set her glass down hard.

Marino's expression was thoughtful. She finally pressed him, "Well... what do you make of it?"

After more pause, he said, "You might just be onto something." She gave a big grin. "But," he cautioned holding up one finger, "you are not allowed to go off on investigating tangents on your own. Our understanding involved you chit-chatting with people at the bar."

Steaming meals were set down in front of them by the waiter.

"Alright, alright. How about we enjoy dinner now?" Dart asked.
Marino shook his head and said "You got it."

Over their meal, they diverted from talk of the case and instead delved into growing up in Baltimore. Dart found herself warming to Marino's deadpan delivery of a story and realized she was actually enjoying herself.

When dinner drew to a close, they walked outside and stood by Dart's car. She suddenly felt nervous. "Well...."

"Alright back to your real job tomorrow right?" Marino said.

She smiled sweetly and said, "Sure...my real job."

Walking away from her, he said, "Don't mess with me Hastings, I mean that."

Chapter Thirteen

When Dart got back to her apartment, Marvin greeted her at the door in a very talkative mood. While getting him fed, the phone rang and Dart gave a jump.

"Five letter word for great," her mother's chirpy voice came through the line.

"Viola," Dart replied without missing a bit.

"Didn't fit."

"What's up?"

"Who are you taking to the banquet tomorrow night?"

"Oh geez, I forgot all about it." The National Congress held a banquet for all the leagues in the area after the season ended. The event was held to honor teams and individuals and the trophies and any additional prize money was formally presented. Dennys Smith presided over the event with much glory. "I was going to go on my own I guess."

"Oh." Silence filled the line.

"You want to go with me to the banquet, Mom?"

"I'd love to honey, thanks for asking."

"No problem. Pick you up at 8?"

Busywork kept Dart occupied the next day. That evening she drove out and picked up Viola who swiftly commented over her choice of outfit. With an inward groan, Dart tried not to regret her choice in dinner partner. Viola chatted throughout the drive to the largest Knights of Columbus Hall in the region situated at about 2 o'clock on the beltway.

Dart usually enjoyed the banquet especially since she knew people across a lot of the leagues. Not much for dating, Dart found herself going to these sorts of occasions stag---or as in the case of this evening, with Viola. Pulling her car into the dimly lit parking lot, she saw that many were already there and the entrance was blazing with lights.

The hall harkened back to earlier era of parties and functions. The ticky tacky interior included a grotto-like fountain in the entry hall complete with light fixtures with simulated torch flames.

Picking up their seat cards, Dart and Viola found their places next to other players from the Citylanes League including Shirl and Larry.

"Hey there ladies," Shirl greeted them. She had made efforts to doll up as evident by the ruby red lipstick applied to her mouth.
"Nice to have you with us Mizz Hastings."

Viola thanked her and asked after her family. Dart turned to the others and greeted them in turn. Larry stood up and pulled chairs out for them with the graciousness of a host. Some other people at the table were from the Paradise Alley League, one of their biggest competitors in the regionals. A barrel chested man from that league came flat out and asked: "So what's the real story behind Holmes' murder?"

Dart's league members looked at each other as if seeking a spokesperson. Before anyone could reply, Viola piped in: "No one really knows the real story, right?" With that, she looked around the table for agreement.

Ralph followed up Viola's comment and said: "I guess we all got our own ideas about the real story."

"What do you mean by that?" Shirl asked sharply.

"Ask Bobby whydontcha?"

"Goddarn Ralph will you get off that kick." Then addressing the whole table, Shirl said: "I don't think anyone's made head nor tails of it."

At that moment, the maitre de invited their table to help themselves to the buffet.

Lines formed on either side of buffet and the food trays contained a mélange that included spiral ham and congealed pasta.

At the table, conversation continued along the same vein about the subject that everyone was now tired of but couldn't stop talking about. Dart finally had enough and turned to the table behind her to ask Miss Ivy if she was enjoying the banquet. Miss Ivy, resplendent in an emerald green mock silk dress that was offset by her trademark hairdo said, "I just can't help but compare it to back in the day when the Congress really put on the ritz. I guess they just can't do that anymore." She accented the thought by poking around with her fork in some cardboard stiff mashed potatoes.

The Congress just like all the alleys was feeling the pinch of the decline of popularity of duckpin. The Congress supported itself by providing sanctioning for the leagues and alleys. Losing sanctioned leagues and sanctioned alleys meant big problems. Dennys Smith was trying his damnedest to beat the odds as the sport diminished and unsanctioned alleys and leagues began to be accepted sullying the whole history of duckpin bowling. This explained his scheme of offering the reward money to keep the revived interest in duckpin piqued.

While the guests were dallying over coffee and desserts, Dennys made his way up to the podium and began to speak about the leagues and their performances. Before getting in too deep, he asked for a moment of silence to respect and honor the memory of Lester Holmes, deceased.

After some long-winded words on the greatness of the sport, the Congress and everybody else, he began the main event: the presentation of awards. Most were predictable. Bobby Blaze did not get the top seated male award which broke his five year streak.

Dennys announced a new category to honor the efforts of those trying to preserve the sport of duckpin bowling in tough economic times. "Let's face it folks, if we don't get customers in the alley, the sport's on its way out. For that reason we have created a new award for the "most profitable league". In other words, the league which has consistently brought in the most money to its respective alley. And that award goes to Miss Ivy Walker!"

Miss Ivy gave the crowd a beautific smile and got to her feet. Slowly she walked up to podium and accepted her award from Dennys. While handing the envelope to Miss Ivy, Dennys announced that the award included a complimentary dinner for herself and a friend with him at Haussner's Restaurant, a Baltimore institution, as Dennys pronounced it.

The crowd applauded loudly with one or two yelling out: "Alright Miss Ivy!" Miss Ivy in turn offered a few words to the audience.

"I'd just like to say that just like every other year I've had a great time with great people. Keep on signing up for the leagues everyone. I'll be calling you for sign up soon enough," she said with a twinkle in her eye.

Everyone at Dart's table laughed affectionately.

"She's such a sweetheart," Larry said.

Dart glanced at Shirl who quickly looked down. Her thoughts were on Shirl's revelations about Miss Ivy. Shirl also appeared to be reflecting on a different Miss Ivy.

Chapter Fourteen

After her day at the races, Dart found herself mixing again with the horsey set of Baltimore. As to be expected in a city with strong Irish roots, there were a number of Garrity's listed in the phone book. Fortunately, one of them was an Alvin Garrity, Jr. Dart had a hunch this Garrity would play out. Instead of calling, she noted the address and took a drive out to a neighborhood outside of the beltway, Sparks.

Al Jr. had seemingly done well for himself judging from his spread in Baltimore's horse country. Dart pulled up a long paved driveway which stopped at a sprawling neo-Colonial house. After knocking on the door, a housewifey looking woman answered.

"Hi", Dart started confidently, "I'm looking for a Mrs. Al Garrity?"

"Yes?" the woman replied in a flat, cold voice.

"I'm working on a special research project for the National Duckpin Bowling Congress. I understand your...husband was one of Baltimore's greats."

"No. It was my father-in-law. He's deceased."

"Oh," Dart attempted to fake a crestfallen expression. "Is your mother-in-law still living?"

"She's not...uh...available."

Dart waited expectantly.

The woman then said in a confiding tone, "She actually has Alzheimer's, and she's in a home down in Ocean City. When she's feeling up to it, she enjoys watching the ocean. But really she would not be any help to you."

"Well, how about your husband?"

"He was just a teenager when his dad died. He doesn't have much recollection of that time period. You're welcome to call him if you like. He works for All State Insurance at their headquarters downtown."

After thanking Mrs. Garrity, Jr., Dart drove home, not knowing if it had been a worthwhile trip or not.

Chapter Fifteen

Dart decided to take some time and clear her head. What better way than a day at the shore in springtime? The mission was two-fold: it would get her out of Baltimore for some stretching room and it would also allow her the opportunity to meet with Garrity's widow.

The drive over to the other shore better known as the Eastern Shore brought pangs of nostalgia with it. Memories of long ago family beach trips flickered between the guardrails of the bridge that spanned the mighty Chesapeake Bay. The trip to the ocean was as familiar as the feel of a duckpin bowling ball.

Dart had got an early start. Even though the summer rush hadn't started yet, the roadways were sometimes clogged up due to bridge improvement projects. Dart had recently heard a report on the news detailing the cost of lead paint abatement on the bridge before actual repainting to the tune of 4 million or so.

Passing by acres and acres of crop land occasionally interrupted by a small town, Dart beat a steady path down to the ocean. By late morning, she could smell the salt air and feel the sticky breeze as she pulled into Ocean City's downtown.

It hadn't been too difficult to track down Mrs. Garrity's rest home. Several phone calls had led to the Surf Villa. Judging from the advertisement she had picked up on the Internet, it was a bit more deluxe than some of the others.

Located on the bay side of Ocean Highway at 121st Street, Surf Villa was spread out among a block or two in a number of tawny colored one story units. A victim of 70s architecture, the place struck a depressing note upon sight.

In the lobby, Dart asked the receptionist for Mrs. Garrity's room. She pointed out in the vague direction of one of the halls that Dart walked down.

Eventually, she hit another desk and was quizzed with a strident tone by a heavy set African American woman in a white uniform, "Can I help you?".

When Dart asked to see Mrs. Garrity, the nurse, whose name tag read 'Rose', looked surprised. "Well, sure, sure. She could stand a visitor or two. Follow me."

The woman waddled toward a room. Opening the door, she said in a higher octave. "Mrs. Garrity, you got company. We don't get much company these days now do we?"

When the attendant moved aside, Dart faced a woman who looked half comatose with some dribble coming out of her mouth. Her skin was almost transculent looking and tissuey. Her hair was severely shorn and grey. She was half sitting up in a recliner chair moving her head around as if looking for something. After a bit, her faded myopic eyes finally focused in on Dart.

She sat up a little taller in her chair and a book dropped out of her lap. Dart bent down to pick it up and noted that it was Curious George, the child's book. Oh boy, she thought to herself, here we go.

"Who are you,"Mrs. Garrity suddenly barked out.

Dart said" Mrs. Garrity, I'm Dart Hastings and I'd like to talk to you about your husband and duckpin bowling."

"My husband? I don't have a husband."

The attendant pulled Dart to the side and whispered: "She gets real agitated when you mention her husband. I'd stay away from that topic if I were you."

Dart moaned to herself. Great. Now what.

She took another stab. "Okay, well what do you know about duckpin bowling?"

"Never heard of him. Who is he?"

"How many children do you have Mrs. Garrity?"

"None. No children. Just cats and dogs. Except...they keep hiding my cats and dogs from me." She focused on the attendant. "Where did you put them? I told you they need me."

"Now, now," Rose answered, "They're with me at the front desk. Just fine."

"Oh...okay." Her agitation diminished some.

Looking back at Dart, she barked. "And you! What do you want?"

"Nothing. Just wanted to visit and say hi."

61

With that response, Mrs. Garrity leaped from her chair with an agility that shocked Dart and grabbed her arm with a death grip attempting to punch her with her free hand.

Rose sprang into action and grabbed Mrs. Garrity yelling above her head, "She can get a little combative in the afternoons."

Dart managed to shrug off Mrs. Garrity and backed out to the entrance of the room.

Rose pushed Mrs. Garrity on the bed and wrestled with her until she finally stopped. At that point, Mrs. Garrity was talking out loud in a run-on stream of consciousness. Dart heard the name Al and moved to the bed to hear more.

"that no good lying cheat mother always said he'd be the death of me him having affairs left and right I told him he better cut it off I didn't want to ever see his bastard child walking up to my front door or her her thinking she could ever get her low class paws on him……."

Dart picked up the gist of it. Leaving Surf Villa, she dissected Mrs. Garrity's words and tried to piece it back together again.

She headed to the boardwalk. Ocean City had prided itself for many years on its well maintained boards which offered the visitor an amazing array of junk food and cheap t-shirts. The food selections included Dolle's salt water taffy, Candy Kitchen fudge, Grottoe's pizza or Dough Roller's pizza (take your pick), Kohr's brothers or Dumser's cones and the list continued. The boards stretched for 26 blocks or so. The southern end of the boardwalk was the location for several ride amusement parks. One of these still had a vintage carousel covered with an oval wooden roof.

Dart gobbled down a slice of pizza purchased at one of the first stands she could find. Sipping on a coke, she walked along the boardwalk her mind deep in thought. She almost bumped into him before he spoke up. "Dart, what's happening?" Billy Blaze sat up on the concrete wall that butted into the boards, legs swinging.

"Billy?" Dart was shocked to see him there. "What…what are you doing here?"

"Oh…just taking a day off. How about you?"

"Uh..the same thing. A day off."

"You meeting anybody down here?"

Billy was nice enough but had always made Dart a little nervous especially since the scene at the alley. She definitely did not want to while the afternoon away with him.

"No, I gotta get back to Baltimore soon." She hesitated before saying. "I'll see you later okay?"

"Sure, sure," Billy grinned in an odd manner.

Now what was going on? Dart felt Billy's eyes on her back as she walked away. Finally, she took a look behind her several hundred feet along and saw that he was indeed staring at her. She felt chills down her back.

What was it about him that made her so nervous? He had always been pleasant enough. He was devoted to Miss Ivy which was certainly admirable to see in anyone. Maybe it was just the prejudicial taint that stuck to single men who never married. As men of his ilk headed into their 40s the taint became more pronounced.

Her mind battled between thinking about the coincidence of running into Billy and thinking about Mrs. Garrity's wild ramblings back at the Surf Villa. As the late afternoon sun made its final dip over the placid shore, she instead turned her mind to the scenery on hand. The dark water etched a sharp contrast with the billowy sky that darkened with the setting of the sun. Dart took in a deep breath of ocean air and headed back to her car.

Chapter Sixteen

Marino faced off with the large man in front of him.

"Alright Bunny. Tell me what you know about Cal Lombard."

Bunny shrugged disinterested. "He hangs out at the track sometimes. There a law against that?"

Marino could see that Bunny had the part of the bored nonplussed sleaze bag down pat. He quickly thought out his best tack for this engagement.

"No, no law against that. Laws against some other things though." He silently stared at Bunny for some moments. Bunny's reaction was to look down at his fingernails and pick at one problem area in particular. Bunny wasn't giving an inch. It was time to bring some bigger guns in. Marino discreetly pressed a buzzer underneath the table.

Tony waltzed through the door and feigned surprise when he saw Bunny.

"Well Bunny what are you doing here?"

Bunny's big form shifted slightly in his chair.

"So Bunny," Tony continued, "You got something to tell me about that deal that went down on Park Heights the other night."

He tilted his head belligerently. "Don't know what you're talking about."

"Oh Bunny I think you do. I got it from a very reliable source if you know what I mean."
Bunny stared at Tony. His eyes were blinking like a rabbit, Marino noted.

In many situations some of the junkies rechanneled alliances particularly if a deal had gone bad and people had gotten hurt or killed. Marino assumed Tony had something on Bunny and Bunny realized it. He waited for the next move as if watching a game of chess.

The next move was Bunny's. He mumbled, "What do you wanna know about Crazy Cal?"

Tony turned to Marino and made a sweeping hand gesture before leaving the room. Marino thought to himself it works like magic everytime. People buy and sell themselves every second of the day.

Marino began his interrogation. "What was the connection between Cal Lombard and Lester Holmes?"

"Lester was a loser. Crazy Cal funded him. I made the connection. I also make the collection."

"Did you kill Lester Holmes?"

Bunny snorted.

"Alright.....who killed Lester Holmes?"

"It wasn't me and it wasn't Crazy Cal. Cal plays a straight game. No funny business or he cuts me out. Makes it real clear."

"Why is Cal "playing" at all? Why doesn't he stick to duckpin bowling alleys?"

"He's a businessman that's why. He doesn't screw around if there's no sense in the deal. That duckpin thing is on its way out anyway."

"So you're telling me it's pure coincidence that Lester bowled at Cal's alley, was heavily in debt to Cal from dealings at the track, and ended up dead at Cal's alley. No coincidence?"

"It's goofy. I can see it from your point but I'm telling you Cal plays a straight game."

"Well, I'll be asking good old "Crazy" Cal about all this."

"Be my guest."

Bunny lifted his heavy frame out of the chair and positioned dark sunglasses back on his face before heading out the homicide unit.

"Bunny...one more thing. Why do you call him Crazy Cal?"

Bunny answered without turning around. "Cuz he's anything but."

Marino sat back at his desk and propped his hands behind his head. While he was sitting there, one of the rookie detectives walked up and took a seat by his desk. "Mister we got problems," he said. "You know that alibi you wanted checked out." Marino nodded his head. He had put the kid on checking out whether Bobby Blaze had really been with his honey the night of Lester's murder or not.

The kid replied: "Well it didn't check out. The toots said she and Bobby are on the outs and she hasn't been with him for quite a while."

"Well that certainly gives us a twist doesn't it? Maybe it's time we pay a visit to Mr. Blaze."

Chapter Seventeen

Dart stared miserably at her computer monitor and felt the heavy weight of inertia. She couldn't get motivated to fill out client reports on insurance cases. Research jobs were her first love but insurance fraud cases were her bread and butter. She had gotten involved in the insurance cases under a mentor several years earlier with the goal of getting out from under and being her own boss. The independence came with a price: the constant shuffle to find new work. Fortunately, her mentor had recently retired and had sent many of his clients her way. She was grateful but she would rather have more research jobs like the one Park Canby had given her.

Marvin was darting around the room chasing sunspots on the hardwood floor. She envied him his ambition.

"You know what, Marvin?" she looked over at the cat to see if he was listening. "Baltimore really is just a small town big city and duckpin bowling is a subculture within it."

Dart couldn't stop thinking about the duckpin research. She perused her list of potential interviewees. She picked up the phone and made an appointment with Mabel Hedges, a lead she had gotten from Fontana Lanes. Mabel was now housebound so Dart arranged to meet her at her house for that afternoon. Mabel had been very enthused about the project and applauded Park Canby for initiating it. She had said she always wanted to do something like this herself.

It only took Dart fifteen minutes to drive up to Randallstown. From that point, she easily located Mabel's house. While waiting for the door to be answered, she noted the neighborhood around her: faded but hanging on to an aura of bourgeoisie. There was an eery stillness to the air. From the other side of the door, she could hear a creaking noise. When the door opened, she understood. Mabel was in a wheelchair and had navigated her way to open the door. A diminutive woman, it appeared that it was taking every bit of her strength to open the door.

"Hello dear. You must be Dart," Mabel offered her hand in greeting, "Come in, come in." Mabel had a wide smile and a startling pair of vibrant green eyes. Her skin was clear revealing blue veins directly beneath the surface. She did not look well.

Once seated in a living room filled with antiques, Dart asked Mabel about her duckpin days.

Mabel's face shined as she spoke of her younger years and the pleasure that duckpin bowling had brought to her life. "Practically every neighborhood had its own alley and it really brought folks together. I was 15 when I started bowling. I remember that first night when Mama gave me some money---just enough for the game and a pop. I felt so grown-up let me tell you."

"So you started competing with the league when you were...?"

"Well let's see I was 18 and that meant I was able to play in the adult league."

"Can you tell me some about the competitions and maybe some of the players?"

"Everyone used to get real worked up about the league competitions. You woulda thought it was the World Series sometimes. I'll tell you...the league manager and the owners would really get everybody going. Then of course the individual competitions were another deal altogether."

"Do you ever play on a league that made it through the regional championships?"

"Yes, I did and it was certainly one of my finest hours. I'll tell you, since getting trapped in this thing," she slapped the wheels of her chair, "I think back more often to those days." Mabel stared off into the distance and Dart waited. "It was 1964 and I was 21. I was playing with two guys from the neighborhood. We swept them. Went all the way to the Congress championships and then to Massachusetts for the nationals. Of course we didn't win the nationals but we gave them a good run."

"Who were the greats?"

"I'll tell you what. Reach up on that bookshelf over there. There should be some scrapbooks..." Dart stood on tip-toes, reaching her arm up she grabbed a hold of the book on top. Wiping off a heavy layer of dust, she handed it over to Mabel.

Mabel pulled on her pince-nez and began to leaf through the yellowed pages making small contented noises.

"Oh look at this...I'm sure you've heard about Al Garrity." Dart nodded. "Well here he is at the 1960 championships. That's a great shot." She pushed the book towards Dart. The photograph depicted Al holding a big trophy over his head with a gleeful expression. Continuing to leaf through the pages, she stopped at one of Miss Ivy and commented, "And for the women I'd have to say Ivy Walker put on quite a show. Then later on Toots Callahan pushed Ivy out of the running. By that time her bad back had kicked in anyway. But for the men...well nobody could quite fill Al's shoes. There were good bowlers don't get me wrong...but..." Mabel green eyes took on a faraway look.

"What was he like as a person?"

"Oh...debonair...I guess that's a good word. We all loved him."

"By all, do you mean ladies and men?"

She gave a chuckle. "I'd have to say the ladies were especially partial to him."

This was a new piece to Al, slightly in contradiction to the newspaper clippings about the devoted family man.

Dart asked a question on a hunch. "Do you think he was loyal to his wife?"

Mabel looked a little flustered. "Dear we didn't have the kind of shenanigans that go on now between folks back then. I'm sure he was....." Her voice, however, did not sound sure.

"What about his death? It sounded awfully suspicious."

"You know, I never believed that story about him drinking. He wasn't ever drunk at any of the functions. There was something fishy about the whole thing."

"Would you mind if I looked through the rest of the book?" Dart asked Mabel.

Mabel handed it over saying "Take your time."

While Mabel continued to wax nostalgic, Dart carefully looked through the clippings. About halfway through, she hit a page that had a copy of the photo that she had found under Miss Ivy's desk. She delicately interrupted Mabel and asked about the photo.

Mabel placed her glasses back on and scrutinized the page. Sighing, she sat back in her wheelchair and took her glasses down. "It's such ancient history I might as well tell you. Just between you, me and the bedpost, Ivy had it something fierce for Al. Him being a married man, you would have thought...well anyway, she tended to make a spectacle of herself at times. On that particular day, she insisted that their picture be taken together. What's funny is that after that picture was taken a tradition was started and the top male and top female were always posed together. I shouldn't talk out of school like that...but I can't help but remember how irritated a lot of us were."

"Why irritated?" Dart asked.

"How can I put this? Like in the ballet they have a prima donna. That's what we had with Ivy." Dart's face must have reflected her surprise because Mabel continued with "I know, I know she's changed a lot, you'd never guess it now... but she was young then like we all were..."

Driving out of Mabel's neighborhood, Dart thought over the conversation. Was she spending too much time on this Al Garrity link? Was it even a link?

Chapter Eighteen

Once Dart finished up at Mabel's, she found herself at loose ends. It was unseasonably humid and her chores were more or less completed so she headed in the direction of Ivanhoes. "What the hell," she told herself.

It was still earlyish but there was a pretty sizeable crowd for a weeknight. She spotted Shirl and Larry at the end of the bar; Shirl was gesticulating wildly and Larry, well, Larry was being Larry. The calm foil to Shirl's exciteability.

Dart made her way towards them. When she reached them, she saw a few others from their league sitting around also. When Dart walked up, Shirl barely managed to nod at her---she was so involved in what she was saying. Dart caught the tail end: "...so when Dennys Smith and his higher-ups catch wind of all this, you better believe there will be hell to pay."

There were nods all around. Shirl paused to take a chug of her beer. She addressed Dart's presence by asking her: "So did you hear?"

Dart responded by looking blank.

"Get a beer girl. You're not going to believe this one." The usually silent Larry said and then gestured towards an open bar stool.

One of the guys hailed Lou over and Dart asked for a draft. Lou hung over their end of the bar listening in after bringing Dart her draft.

Shirl began to fill Dart in. Eyes gleaming, she practically rubbed her hands together as she told Dart the latest in duckpin scandal. Kenny Wallingford and Randall Roper, two fairly decent players in their league, had decided to try their luck in an away tournament. The national tournament was held in Boston after each season. Even though they weren't the highest scorers in their league, it was possible for them to sign up and be matched with equivalent competition in the nationals. It was unusual given the expense involved but it did happen.

As luck would have it, Randall won a game. When he went to collect the money, he discovered that they did not have Citylanes listed as a sanctioned alley. Because of this, he was not able to collect his winnings.

Part of the nightly take that Miss Ivy had collected from all of them had supposedly gone towards sanctioning the alley and providing for its membership in the National Duckpin Bowling Congress. What this meant was that Miss Ivy had not used the money for that purpose.

Dart was flabbergasted. She asked: "Why would Miss Ivy do such a thing?"

Joey piped in with: "The color of money, babe, the color of money."

"Wait. Are you saying that Miss Ivy pocketed the money?"

Shirl looked askance. Dart remembered too late the under the table winnings that she had hinted a few select players were involved in. Is that where the money went?

Dart's question hung in the air before Ralph, Lester's teammate, said: "All I know is that Randall is fit to be tied. He's not going to let this baby go to bed. He's getting Dennys Smith involved and the whole nine yards." He finished by taking a drag on his cigarette.

"Well, has anybody confronted Miss Ivy?" Dart asked.

"Sure, sure," Ralph replied, "Randall went over there first thing. She denies the whole thing. Says they must have 'misplaced' the sanction application." He shook his head in disgust. "First Lester, now this..." Dart was taken aback. How were the two incidents possibly related?

Joey snorted. "Just because a dame gets some age on her don't mean we have to listen to her lies."

"Ain't that the truth," Larry chimed in.

Everybody looked at him in surprise. If this had gotten under Larry's skin, it was pretty bad.

As Dart sipped on her beer, she made a mental note to check in with Dennys Smith.

Chapter Nineteen

Dart placed a call to Dennys Smith's office the next morning. The number for the Congress was 1-800-DUC-KPIN. Catchy. A prerecorded message picked up and gave a series of suggestions before finally offering the alternative of talking to a live person. After Dart pressed that digit, she was bestowed with an earful of MUSAK---Neil Diamond soulfully singing "Sweet Caroline".

A receptionist eventually (and regretfully judging from her tone of voice) came on the line. "Can I help you?" she asked.

"Dennys Smith please."

"Who's calling?"

"Dart Hastings."

"Does he know what this is in reference to?"

"He knows me. He'll take the call." Dart was abruptly put back on MUSAK after saying that. Diamond was belting out "good times never seemed so goo—ood!".

Dennys' voice cut through the line. "Dart! What a pleasure. How may I be of service?"

Dart felt an unpleasant shiver run through her. There was something about Dennys' voice that was...whiny. It reminded her of something but she couldn't think what.

"Hello, Dennys. What's going on with the sanctioning bit at Citylanes?"

"Oh that." Dennys lowered his voice. "After some investigation, it appears that Miss Ivy..um...didn't quite understand the sanction rules this year."

"Have you asked her where the money got to?"

"That's out of my purview. Something for Miss Ivy and the league folks to work out." Dart had a mental image of Dennys literally wiping his hands to rid himself of further involvement.

"Okay. What is within your 'purview'?"

"The Congress will be sending out---regretfully---a letter of reprimand to Miss Ivy. A kind of reminder about her responsibilities to the league and the alley. The letter will be signed by Cal Lombard, as the alley owner, and myself."

"You and Cal Lombard got quite the partner thing going on there."

"Cal has been a terrific support to the Congress since buying Citylanes. You ought to realize that Dart. Didn't you see him at the banquet the other night?"

Dart said thoughtfully, "Yeah, I guess I did."

"Well, if there's nothing else..."

Dart reluctantly ended the conversation---feeling like maybe she hadn't asked the right questions while she had Dennys on the string. A letter of reprimand? Well, it wasn't like the National Duckpin Congress was a court of law or a tribunal. What did she expect anyway? An organization was only as good as those that participated in it.

Maybe Miss Ivy was getting a little befuddled. She was getting on in years. But that didn't jive with Shirl's hinting that there was some off betting on the league. Miss Ivy would still have to keep her wits sharpened to handle the high finances of that pool.

Dart couldn't reconcile all of this to the image she had of Miss Ivy. The woman who graciously talked about the old days of duckpin in the community. The woman who sat sweetly at the desk while the league members jostled and jibed at each other during game nights. The woman who cared deeply for people in her neighborhood as evidenced by the close relationship she had with two kids that grew up near her, the Blaze twins.

There was probably a reasonable explanation, and Dart would find out what.

Chapter Twenty

Dart had a message on her machine the next day from Shirl. Randall Roper was calling all the league members together. The meeting was at Ivanhoe's that night. Short notice, Dart thought, but then again South Baltimorons had their own sense of time.

Out of pure curiosity, Dart decided to attend the impromptu meeting. She got there late. League members were sitting in the corner around a big round table, a table that Lou generally reserved for the older patrons. As she approached, she saw angry expressions and heard some heated tones. She guessed that the discussion had probably been going on for awhile. But then again it didn't take much to fire this group up.

Dart took a quick survey of the crowd. Conspicuously absent were the Blaze twins. Otherwise the league was well-represented. She grabbed a chair and pulled it towards the group.

She caught some of what Wally was saying: "....so I say we go over there and confront her. All of us at once." A couple of others nodded and murmured assent with Wally's plan.

Randall put his hands up. "No, no, no. The point of this isn't to intimidate old ladies. There's got to be another solution."

The usually quiet Larry jumped in the conversation. "I've got an idea." Everyone looked at each other then at Randall.

Randall said: "Well sure Larry. Speak up."

"It's pretty simple. Appoint a representative and then have that rep go to Dennys Smith and Cal Lombard and tell them we want a new league manager."

The crowd took a collective pause. As Larry had said, it was a simple plan but ironically no one had put it to the floor yet.

Discussion ensued amongst everyone. Dart, seated a little behind and to the left of Shirl, leaned forward. "Shirl...psst," she said.

Shirl turned around. "Oh hey girl. Didn't see you back there."

"Do you think everyone's being fair to Miss Ivy? This job means everything to her."

"Well, Shirl paused. "It's not like we're asking for her not to run the alley. We're only saying she can't be league manager no more."

Dart lowered her voice. "Shirl..what if she fingers you and the others about the betting deal?"

Shirl squirmed in her seat. "Never you mind about that. Neighborhood people don't do that kind of thing to each other. No matter what."

Randall was getting the crowd's attention once again. "From what I'm hearing, it sounds like Larry's hit the nail on the head and this is what we need to."

Dart had to hand it to Randall. He was really facilitating this well. But then if she remembered correctly, his day job was that of union rep. Mediation was the name of the game.

Randall continued. "And as Larry suggested, it would be good to get one rep to speak for all of us. Any ideas?"

Kenny, a biggish guy with arms like slabs of beef, said: "Well it's gotta be you Randall, don't it?"

Randall shook his head. "No, this has to be about the group not just what happened to me. Otherwise, they'll think I'm driving this train."

Somebody guffawed and said: "Well you are, aren't ya?"

Larry cut in: "No this is about all of us and what's fair and right. If we're paying those dues for league sanctioning that's what it goes for."

Again, there was general surprised reaction to Larry saying his piece.

Randall looked thoughtful. "You know I'm thinking Larry should be our spokesman."

Shirl clapped Larry on the back. "Yeah, me too."

After a quick vote, it was unanimous.

As the crowd was breaking up, Dart approached Larry.

"Larry, I got to say I'm surprised you're getting so involved in this."

"You know Dart, I'm surprised too. But this really burns me up. It's just not right."

Dart had a brief flashback to Bobbby Blaze and Lester Holmes during the last game of the season. After Lester had heckled Bobby, Bobby had reeled on him and said the exact same words: "It's just not right."

Dart focused back in on Larry. "I know just what you mean, Larry."

Driving home, Dart reviewed the session that had taken place. She was reminded of an occasion years back. She had held an office job in a small company. The owner had decided that they needed a communications retreat. The retreat was held off-site for one day and run by a facilitator. Behind the boss's back everyone had referred to it as a "touchy-feely session". The objective of the day had been for everyone to get to know each other's communication styles and hence, in understanding those styles, the office would become a well-oiled machine based on communication dynamics. The theory did have its merits but in practice humans were another sort of animal altogether. Within the first day back, the usual sparring and petty back-talk continued without a bump in the road.

Dart had however learned a few tricks from the facilitator. A woman from Texas with a brassy blonde hairdo, made-up to perfection, and about 5 foot tall, the facilitator had been a treat to watch in action. She had managed to be as sweet as honey while at the same time held the course with a steely undercurrent. The point of the matter was that a group could work things out if given a reasonably attainable goal. Randall was seemingly on the right track with his attempt to better the league. Even though he had personally been burned, he was now pursuing the good of the whole. And his talents at mediation came into the foreground.

Dart's only hope was that Miss Ivy would not get hurt too badly because of this. Maybe she should try to talk to Miss Ivy herself. There could be a reasonable explanation for all of it. She resolved to go to Citylanes and talk to Miss Ivy the next day.

Chapter Twenty-One

Dart sifted through her mail the next day. In addition to an outrageously high bill from the Baltimore Gas and Electric Company and a promotion for yet another credit card, Dart was copy furnished on a letter from the National Duckpin Congress. Apparently, Dennys Smith had copied all the league members on the "official" letter that he had sent to Miss Ivy. It was a very bland letter that basically expressed that, "in the future, all monies collected for sanctioning are to be programmed for sanctioning not any other league business." "Other league business"? What the hell was that Dart thought. Miss Ivy had gotten off pretty easy and Dart had the feeling that this wasn't going to sit well with the league members at all.

She re-read the letter while gulping down a quick breakfast of orange juice and toast. She decided it was time to pay that visit to Citylanes.

The door to Citylanes was open and Dart galloped up the stairs to Miss Ivy's office. Approaching the doorway, Dart could see from the outline of crossed legs in the chair opposite Miss Ivy that she had a visitor.

As she got closer, Dart recognized the profile of Cal Lombard. Even though she had only encountered him once or twice, his distinct features and his close cropped silver hair made him easily recognizable.

Both Miss Ivy and Cal looked up when Dart walked in. Dart sensed that she was interrupting a private conversation. Her eyes glanced over the desk where there was a piece of stationary laying open. Even from the distance she could make out the large flourish of a signature that was Dennys Smith. Dart could guess what the topic of conversation had been.

"Oh so sorry. I didn't realize you had company," she began.

Miss Ivy had an annoyed expression on her face but Cal jumped in before Miss Ivy could reply. "Not at all Ms. Hastings. Not at all." While talking he had risen to his feet and proffered a delicately manicured hand for Dart to shake.

There was an awkward silence and then Miss Ivy cleared her throat. "Something you needed Dart?"

"I wanted to talk to you...but if it's a bad time..."

Cal interjected with: "Why don't you pull a chair in and we can all chat."

Dart looked at Miss Ivy who became increasingly more uncomfortable judging from her body language as she shuffled papers to and fro the top of her desk. But Dart grabbed a chair from outside the office and pushed herself next to Cal.

"So…" Cal started, "I understand there's some discontentment among some of the league members."

"Yeah, I'm sure you've heard all about it from Dennys…actually the reason I'm here is..well I thought that if they heard some sort of reasonable explanation they might all back down a little."

Miss Ivy continued to nervously fidget. Cal responded: "Oh but you see Miss Hastings there's nothing to back down from." He gestured towards Dennys' letter and said, "The letter covers it all. There was a bit of misunderstanding and it won't happen again. Right, Ivy?"

Miss Ivy answered sheepishly. "Right."

"I don't want to speak for the group but I don't think that's going to be enough."

Cal looked straight at Dart and raised his eyebrows. "I beg to differ young lady. It will be enough."

Dart was taken aback. She had the sinking feeling that Cal Lombard was used to getting what he wanted and that the "protest" would end with Dennys' letter. Feeling as though she had just been handed her walking papers, Dart fumbled around for some parting lines and then beat a hasty retreat.

Chapter Twenty-two

At Ruth's House of Coffee, Dart waited impatiently for a cappuccino to go. She had an appointment with an insurance client and she needed this morning jumpstart. Nine in the morning was a little too early for her blood. Especially since it didn't include cigarettes these days. Unfortunately, others felt the same judging from the line that weaved from the entrance to the small counter. She sighed deeply and tried to dip into her limited patience reserves.

Her irritation was suddenly interrupted by a light tap on her shoulder. She turned to see Wally. Standing there with a steaming cup of coffee. Staring at the cup with envy, Dart exchanged hellos. Then she said: "I never took you for someone that goes to coffee houses."

"What'd you mean---I'm not yuppie enough?"

Dart thought to herself, Try not yuppie at all. Out loud she said: "No nothing like that. Just...well, you seem like more of a tea drinker."

"Huh?," Wallie had a perplexed look on his face. Then he said: "I guess I just really needed the caffeine after what went down last night. This league crap is getting too deep for me."

"What happened now?" Dart asked.

"It was all over Ivanhoe's last night. Randall sold out."

"Sold out? How do you mean?" Dart was keeping one eye on the line as it slowly crawled closer to her finish line.

"He passed the word along that he was satisfied with Dennys' letter and told everybody to just let the whole thing drop. He doesn't want to deal with it anymore."

This was definitely an about face on Randall's part. "So who do you think he sold out to?"

"Wallinger was there. He thinks Lombard got to Randall. Made him pipe down. Everybody was pretty disgusted last night."

Dart could imagine the scene. So much for the great dynamics that Randall had established for the league. Dart was sure the whole thing had fragmented pretty quickly. She asked Wallie: "Does anybody want to keep pressing the matter?"

Wallie rubbed his free hand over his unshaven face. "Nah, we all got pretty wasted and by the end of the night nobody was really talking about anymore. Hey...I got to get to the construction site. See you 'round." With that, Wallie lumbered out of the shop. Dart stared after him. Oh well she thought. She was now one deep from getting her beverage of choice and started to focus in on the holy experience.

Later, as she drove up to the northern part of the city she thought about Cal Lombard. He had clearly stepped in as Miss Ivy's protector of sorts. Just stopping at defending her actions. Why would he do that? Merely backing up an employee's word? Or was there more to it...

Chapter Twenty-three

"Marino, you got a call on line 3," the receptionist bellowed in a voice larger than her person.

"Yeah, Marino, here."

"Mr. Marino, this is Cal Lombard."

Marino sat up straighter in his chair. "Well Mr. Lombard what a coincidence. I was going to give you a call myself. You saved me a dime."

"Actually, I saved the city government that dime or 35 cents as the case might be but let's not quibble over the small stuff. I'd like for you to meet me at Down the Hatch---it's a little place up near Belvedere Square. Do you know it?"

"I'm sure I can find out. What time?"

"Oh---well right now. I'm here right now."

Marino smiled wryly to himself. Mr. Lombard like all the "monied" people assumed that all were at their beck and call.

"No problem. I'll be there in 20 minutes."

Cutting through uptown, Marino navigated to York Road and drove a couple miles before ending up in the area. The bar was easily located and marked by a big sign with a neon design of a man swallowing a drink.

The bar was dark and narrow. Lombard was one of the only patrons and sat at a corner table. When Marino approached the table, Cal looked up from his drink and said: "Have a seat, Detective."

Marino took the seat offered and studied the man in front of him. Cal had deep circles under his eyes and his Bahamian tan was turning sallow.

"Something to drink?" Cal asked politely.

Marino shook his head, waiting.

Cal cut to the chase."I understand there may be some things you want to talk to me about."

"Word is you have some interests at the track. You wanna tell me more?" Marino asked Cal.

Cal sighed heavily. "Interests? Is that what they're called?"

Marino raised his eyebrows and waited.

"I'm a businessman, Detective. I've always been a businessman. I know no other livelihood and frankly at this point in my life I'm too tired to learn anyway." He took a slow gulp from what appeared to be a makeshift martini before continuing. "My problem has been that I dabble. Dabbling tends to create a deficit in the portfolio."

"So you turned to the track."

"I didn't turn to the track. I never left. I've just upped my, as you call them, "interests" there. It's like a government job. The money's steady and dependable."

"Oh I don't think a government job has the same kind of ambiance."

"Perhaps you're right. Nevertheless, that's what I do. It's a clean operation; no harm nor foul comes to anyone. You can trust my word on it."

"What about the alley? And the reward money?"

"Citylanes has been one of my dabbling adventures. It was a fun sort of a nostalgic trip for me as I used to be quite the duckpin bowler myself." He smiled as if recalling a far off memory. "But it can't go on much longer. I'm liquidating the alley and all its equipment. Shipping it off to the Phillipines next month. There's quite the boom over there with duckpin bowling, did you know?"

Marino shook his head and didn't hold back a look of disgust. "Way to sell out on America Cal."

Cal shrugged and replied "As I said earlier... I'm a businessman. I have to stay in the running. Protect other interests."

"Yeah, other interests. So what's with Lester Holmes? He owed you a lot of money and then he's found dead at your bowling alley. You tell me."

"I'm as baffled as you. Bunny may have pressed him for payment a bit but nothing like that I can assure you."

83

"Can you?"

"I wasn't even in town Detective. I was at my little place in the Bahamas. Also, speaking objectively, wouldn't it be a tad obvious if I had him killed and left him in my alley."

"Who does that leave then?"

"I honestly don't know and," looking down at his watch, "I'm sorry but this conversation is finished."

Marino grunted and said, "Don't run off to the islands anytime soon."

Cal smiled. "I'll put you in touch with my lawyer on that point." He got up from the table and walked away lightly swinging a tortoiseshell umbrella.

Marino continued to sit at the table. The gray lines were blurry. Was Cal a crook? And what about the reward money?

Marino wondered what all of Cal's society friends here and in the Bahamas would think of Cal's business dealings. It was considered usury in some parts of the world. But again lines were blurred as to what was wrong, right or indifferent.

Same with adultery. When his wife had started screwing around on him with a guy she met at her part-time retail job, he had been indignant and self-righteous. She was wrong, he was right. Seven years later, he still struggled through thoughts about why she had done it, if he had pushed her to do it and was it really so wrong as he thought. Shades of grey. That had become the running theme throughout his life, work, personal and otherwise. What was more noble, justice or indifference. It was becoming harder and harder to distinguish.

Chapter Twenty-four

Dart had called Orv Haskin earlier in the day and set up to meet him that afternoon. He had sounded distracted on the phone not really tuning in to the conversation. But, she reflected, maybe it was just his phone manner. Some people were different in person than on the phone. The interviewing phase of her research jobs had taught her that if nothing else.

Arriving at the Fontana this time, she pulled her car into a deserted parking lot except for an old El Camino, vintage late 70s. She assumed it was Orv's car. The day was overcast and played into the emptiness of the lot and the unlit neon sign. Shrugging to herself, she knocked on the door and peeked through the glass. A light was on in the back.

A few moments later she knocked on the door again, no answer. "Maybe he can't hear from back there," she thought. Jiggling the doorknob, she found it unlocked. She walked in.

Calling out Orv's name, she headed toward the light in the back coming from his office. At the doorway, she stopped in her tracks. Orv Haskin was lying faceup, eyes open with a trickle of blood coming from his mouth. Riveted by the sight, she heard something in the background finally realizing it was her screaming. The screams seemed to echo off the corrugated tin walls of the warehouse building.

Frantically, she grabbed for his wrist but felt no pulse. Scrambling for the phone, she picked it up with shaky hands and dialed for help.

Marino carried over a cup of water to Dart who sat on one of the alley's benches. "Here, take a sip," he said.

She sipped while staring straight on.

"First time you see a dead body, it's tough."

She looked at him and asked: "Frankly, I hope it always is."

The alley was now swarming with people getting the necessary information. After the medics had arrived, they had called the police because of suspected foul play. Marino, hearing that the body was at a duckpin alley, had called it for his own. To his surprise, Dart had been on the scene. He had reamed her out before realizing a little too late the circumstances once she burst into tears.

A rookie walked up to Dart and Marino and said: "Blunt instrument to the head. Sound familiar?"

Marino directed him to get a forensics on the wound and possible weapon.

He turned to Dart. "So tell me what you're doing here?"

Dart carefully replayed the events before her arrival.

Marino asked, "Who knew you were coming here?"

Dart shrugged. "Nobody...I generally don't report into anybody about my day to day activities---although my mother would probably like it differently."

Marino stroked his chin as though stroking a beard. Taking a deep breath he turned to Dart and said: "Look, Dart, you're getting a little too close to the fire here. Somebody used you to find Orv's body. Somebody who's a couple steps ahead of the rest of us. Do you understand me?"

Dart shook her head.

"As of now, I don't want you to have anything to do with Lester's case or this one. You've been real helpful but it's time to play hardball with this character whoever it is."

"I'm onto to something though Marino. I can almost taste it...."

"No. You've become an overly enthusiastic amateur sleuth. Detective novels are written about you by the handful." She tried to voice protest but he continued on. "You're going to have to back off, that's all there is to it."

"I'll back off but who's to say whoever used me this time won't try to use me again."

Marino looked at her a couple of seconds before replying. "No one."

Chapter Twenty-five

Dart was finally given the okay to go home. She was feeling a bit wobbly as she headed to her car. As if she had just finished doing a lot of push-ups, or as if she hadn't quite woken up yet.

Once home, a long hot soak in the tub separated Dart from the rest of the world. The only thing distracting her was Marvin meowing for food—or companionship. It was hard to tell. The problem was that every time she tried to close her eyes and relax a vision of Orv Haskins with his bleary eyes looking back at her flashed through her brain.

What had she known about Orv? She tried to cull through the brain cells and remember. He seemed an average Joe, devoted to duckpin bowling as many of his contemporaries.

The phone ringing brought her out of her reverie. The machine clicked on and the familiar tones of Miss Ivy's voice came through.

"Dart, it's Ivy Walker. I called because I heard about today. I feel so badly for you. You've been so helpful to me since everything with Lester happened. Look, I got that dinner with the Congress and I'd…I'd like to take you as my guest. Call me back and let me know."

Dart thought about it. If she went, it would give her opportunity to ask Miss Ivy about Garrity. And the sanctioning stuff could be the left on the shelf for the night.

Dialing Citylanes number, she got Miss Ivy on the first ring. "Hey, it's Dart. I just got home," she fibbed, "Dinner sounds great."

"Good! Now, I know it's short notice but it's for tomorrow night. Dennys was real busy and it was the only time he could fit it in."

Dart smiled wryly at that comment. She was sure that Dennys made sure to create the impression that he was "real busy".

They arranged to meet the following night.

~~~~~~

Dart picked up Miss Ivy at her house. The street of tiny rowhouses gave off a grimy glow. As they pulled away from the block, Miss Ivy pointed out the house where the Blaze twins lived, two doors down from her own.

"They still live together?" Dart questioned.

"Yeah, they're bachelors. No families of their own yet. It'll happen." Miss Ivy added: "They're good boys."

Dart had not realized how close to Miss Ivy the twins lived. They were a tight little group, not unlike a family themselves.

They drove into the eastern part of the city to the restaurant. Miss Ivy had set up to meet Dennys Smith there.

Haussner's was a venerable, Baltimore restaurant known in parts way beyond Baltimore. The exterior with its painted beigeish yellow brick, dentilled cornice, shuttered second story windows, and glassed in entry, gave no clues to the holdings inside. The interior was devoted to one all-encompassing theme: art. Paintings covered every square inch of wall space. The owners had collected artwork from around the world for decades and displayed it in this venue.

Seated at a table for three, Dart and Miss Ivy perused the catalogue style menu while waiting for Dennys. An elderly waitress in a white clinical outfit with matching shoes from another era came up to the table. "Drinks, ladies?" she asked.

Miss Ivy looked at Dart. "Why not," she said, "The Congress is picking up the tab."

Looking at the waitress, she said "How about a Rob Roy for me. And Dart?"

"I'll have a bourbon and branch water."

Dennys made his way to the table out of breath and blustery. "Apologies all around, ladies. Got stuck on a call I just couldn't get away from..." Dart and Miss Ivy murmured the niceties. Once Dennys was settled and had placed a drink order, he turned to Dart and leaned forward: "Dart, tell all. What happened with Orv?" His eyes bore into hers and his curiosity seemed more than idle.

Miss Ivy interjected: "Dennys, she probably wants to put that behind her. Why don't we talk about something more pleasant?"

Dart said: "Thanks Miss Ivy...I guess I would like to put it aside this evening. We're really here for you. You really deserve this dinner. You've worked really hard to keep Citylanes afloat." It almost seemed like lying not to bring up the sanctioning business but, as Miss Ivy had said, it was time for more "pleasant" talk.

Dennys followed with "Here, here," while raising his glass of scotch for a toast.

Miss Ivy sighed and said: "You know, I've done what I can. I know in my heart though that we'll never see the glory days that I once knew at the alleys."

Dennys replied: "Oh let's not dwell on any negativity. We're here to eat, drink and be merry."

Over oxtail soup and then sauerbraten, Miss Ivy regaled Dart and Dennys with tales from the good old days. She spoke of a bygone era that was chock full of duckpin bowling romance. Dart encouraged her reminiscences by asking her questions. "You know I've always been curious about the name. What have you heard?"

Miss Ivy replied: "There were a couple different stories about the name. One story was that Wilbert Robinson and John McGraw, the founders, were duck hunters and saw that when the ball hit the pins it looked like a flock of flying ducks. Another story was that Robinson named duckpin because the pin's shape reminded him of a duck."

Miss Ivy talked on about a lot of the league shenanigans of the 60s and the good times she had enjoyed. Finally a bitter note crept into her voice: "It's different now. Not as friendly. People just don't know how to have a good time anymore."

Dennys, by this time on his second scotch, nodded in agreement.

Shifting his girth in his seat, he adeptly asked: "Well what about poor Orv Haskins? Why would something like this happen? Anybody in the neighborhood talking?"

Miss Ivy shrugged. "Haven't heard nothing down at the alley. We're all still talking about Lester, truth be told."

Dart leaned forward into the conversation. "Did either of you know that there was a connection between Orv and Lester Holmes?"

Dennys raised his eyebrows. Miss Ivy spoke first. "Sure, sure…Lester used to bowl out of the Fontana, right?"

"That's right. What do you remember about those two that might connect the murders, Miss Ivy?"

Miss Ivy seemed to gaze off into space. Finally, she said: "Bowling, that's it. There's no other connection."

Dennys' eyes gleamed and he seemed to relish this new information. He was a little too interested in this, Dart thought to herself. Or was it the sensationalism of it all in an otherwise dull landscape of league politics?

Dart took a deep breath and decided to change the subject. She asked: "Did you know somebody named Al Garrity?"

Miss Ivy looked up startled. "Wha..t?"

"Oh, I was reading some old duckpin news guide and it mentioned him as one of the greatest male bowlers of all times. I just wondered if you had known him."

Miss Ivy said in an irritated tone: "Well, of course I knew him. We played next to each other for ten years. Him always winning the men's, me the ladies." She worked a piece of the tablecloth back and forth.

"Just wondering....what was he like?"

Miss Ivy seemed agitated and answered: "I don't know! He was just one of the boys. Nothing special."

"Hhhmmm. I saw a photograph---he looked pretty special." Dart badgered.

Miss Ivy decisively put down her napkin. "I think it's time to go Dart. I want to go home."

"Miss Ivy, are you okay?"

"You're...you're stirring up some thoughts I don't want to think about."

Dennys interrupted: "Now, now ladies. Try to sit back and relax." But the dinner mood had changed and Miss Ivy was insistent on being driven home.

Dennys told them everything was taken care of and walked them to the door. He himself drifted off into the Stag Bar, right inside the entrance foyer, Dart assumed, for some more libation. Dart peeked her head in the door and immediately took note of the ancient sign "Women not allowed".

"Oh geez look at that." Dart pointed it out to Miss Ivy as she shrugged into her coat with a lackluster attempt to divert Miss Ivy's attention from the earlier heated conversation.

Miss Ivy looked up and said: "You don't know how it was like in them days. You just don't know."

Dart got the feeling the Miss Ivy was speaking of more than just the Stag Bar.

Chapter Twenty-six

Dart sat in Ruth's the next morning with an oversize mug of cappucino steaming up into her face. With pen and pad in front of her, she attempted to sort through everything going on. After some scribbling, she reached the unfortunate conclusion that she was chasing a series of dead ends and loose threads leading to nowhere.

LESTER DEAD.

ORV DEAD.

CAL LOMBARD MAIN MAN AT TRACK.

AL GARRITY + MISS IVY????

BOBBY DRUNKEN.

BILLY WEIRD.

GAMBLING AT CITYLANES.

A cough interrupted her scribblings and she looked up to see Marino standing over her. "How did you know I was here?" she demanded.

He faked a Bogart and said "We have our methods sweetheart."

Dart cringed at the bad Bogart imitation and then realized something. "Wait a minute. You're having me tailed, aren't you?"

Marino replied: "Tailed is a bit antiquated of an expression. We prefer to use the term 'followed'. Anyway, I'm here to go over a few points with you."

"Well...good. Actually, that's exactly what I'm doing right now."

Dart stared down at the notes she had been writing. Suddenly, it struck her. "I totally forgot." She looked up at Marino. "Lester and Orv had a connection."

"What kind of connection? Not a love connection..."

"Come on, Marino. No, nothing like that. But Lester bowled at Orv's alley back in the 60s. He was the closest Orv's alley came to the big-time." Dart went on to explain to Marino some basic duckpin politics. If Lester had competed and

92

won big in the Nationals, his victory would also be, in part, the victory of the alley with which he was associated. He would have essentially put Orv's alley "on the map".

Marino digested all of it then asked: "Why didn't he continue to stay with that alley even if he hadn't won? Wouldn't he have remained loyal to Orv?"

"I don't know," Dart replied, "They could have had a falling out and maybe there was bad blood between them. I interviewed Orv and he was real smooth. Quite the politician."

Marino took a bite out a chocolate chip muffin in front of Dart. "What you need to do is get with the Ivanhoe's crowd. Delicately. Don't raise any eyebrows."

"Got it, chief. Here---have a muffin for the road." She handed him the bitten-into muffin as he stood to leave the coffee house.

Chapter Twenty-seven

It was a slow night at Ivanhoe's. Dart sipped her beer and studied the racing papers that Lou had left on the bar. Racing...what was it about that pastime that sucked people in and left no prisoners? She had always enjoyed going to the track herself but she couldn't see making a religion out of it---or worse, a pact with the devil. She thought about Lester...and Orv. Was their passion for the track behind it all? And if so, why would they ever take it to the nth degree?

The door crashed open and Dart looked up. Bobby was stumbling his way over to her. "Oh geez," she thought, "Here we go again."

"Daaartt," he bellowed in greeting as only a drunk can do effectively.

"Hey, Bobby. Where have you been?"

"I's making the rouns," he slurrred.

Lou came up with a steaming mug of coffee in hand. "Here, Bobby. Sip it down."

When he tried to hand it to Bobby, he swung his arm across the bar knocking the coffee, Dart's beer and the racing form to the ground.

Lou exploded. "That's it. Outta here Bobby. I've had enough of this shit." He marched back into the kitchen, Dart presumed to get cleaning supplies.

Bobby scrambled around on the floor trying to pick up pieces.

"Here. It's all better." He handed the pieces to Dart.

"Bobby, Bobby...what has gotten into to you lately? You've been drunk out of your head every time I see you."

"What's gotten into me? I'll tell you whas gotten into me." He paused rubbing a hand over his eyes. Then as if speaking to himself he said, "Can't tell, can't tell, can't tell." With that, he lurched off the barstool and made his exit.

When Lou came back out, he shook his head at Dart in disgust. "What the hell's with him anyway? Next time I'm going to call that brother of his so he can make himself useful for a change."

"What do you mean by 'for a change' Lou?"

"Ah, I don't know. Something about the guy bugs me. I've never been able to put my finger on it.   And the way he's all over Miss Ivy all the time. It's weird you know?"

Dart thought back to her recent encounters with Billy and how they had unnerved her. "He's different all right,"she said to Lou.

What did Bobby mean by "can't tell"? Was it just drunk talk or...Dart idly picked up the racing form again. She liked to read the horse name's. As she worked her way through the form, she came upon the listing for the Maryland Million, a big deal race to be held that weekend. One of the horses racing was "Goombay Smash". Owner: Cal Lombard. She put the paper down. It might be interesting to observe Cal in his element.

Chapter Twenty-eight

The day of the Maryland Million was overcast and bitter. Dart had to talk herself out of burrowing deeper into the covers and forgetting the whole race idea.

She was going to the race alone. It was better that way in case any sleuthing opportunities presented themselves. And the reality was that there wasn't anyone she really wanted to spend time with....she had a half-hearted idea to call and ask Marino but thought better of it. After battling parking and paying her fare into the grandstand area, she was finally inside and walked around to take in the sights.

As with any other day at the track, people from all walks of life came to the event. She passed by people who probably didn't have a pot to piss in but had somehow managed to get to this race and place bets.

Dart had already picked out her winners from the racing form at Lou's the previous day. She went ahead and placed her bets for ten races. It was going to be a long day. She had wrestled with whether to bet on Lombard's horse or not. It was a long shot---a bay mare who had never raced on turf, 2 ½ years old. But you never knew---sometimes the long shots paid off. She also had the feeling that Cal only dealt with the winners in this life.

The races began and the tension in the crowd heightened and then deflated before and then after each race. In between races they had entertainment such as Jack Russell Terrier dog racing and clowns and mimes. The entertainment however was a mere backdrop to the business at hand---the races and the betting. The undertone of the day was almost palpable: people were there to win, to make money. When that didn't happen, things got tense.

When Dart walked through the grandstand to the rest rooms, she passed by a scraggly bearded man crushing a ticket in his hand staring open-mouthed at the monitor. In the bathroom, she encountered heavy set women with t-shirts stretched across voluminous bosoms and jeans straining at the hips to break free. On her way back, she observed old people dressed in outdated attire hobbling through the crowds. Every time she came to the track, she was fascinated by "the scene".

Finally it was time for the fifth race, the one in which Cal Lombard's horse was racing. Dart positioned herself close to the fence surrounding the winner's circle so that she could catch a view of Cal if he was in attendance.

As the horses pranced by the spectators on their way to the starting gate, everyone began to assemble for the fifth race. And, sure enough, Cal Lombard made his way to the front where all the horse owners and trainers gathered to watch the races that they had a part in.

Cal was smiling as he made his way through the crowds stopping periodically to say hello or kiss a lady on the cheek. On his arm was a buxom blonde approximately 35 years younger than him. It was quite a sight. The woman was obviously class from the salon tint of her blond hair to the expensive Irish moss linen dress with matching jacket that she wore. Dart was close enough to observe that her jewelry, while unobtrusive, was also tastefully expensive. Who was she? Cal's "tart"? She was monied that was for sure. So why would she need a rich sugar daddy if she already came from money? People and their choices never ceased to amaze Dart.

The horses were lined up and the race began. It was a longer race----2 furloughs around the track. Anticipation built in the crowd as the favorites were left in the dust and overtaken by those that the odds were against, including Goombay Smash, Cal's horse. As they made the approach to the finish line, Goombay Smash made a final tear passing Dark Lady and claimed first place. Dart found herself cheering with some others in the crowd. She had won big. 10-1 odds on a $2 bet to win. Not bad for a day at the track.

Down in the winner's circle, Cal and the blonde were hugging as others clapped Cal on the back. The second and third place winners were also in the circle and everyone appeared quite pleased with themselves. The ladies all had on hats or bonnets along with other finery. The men were all dressed in rich looking suits and carried pipes or other props. The contrast between the rest of the lot in the grandstand with these folks was marked. The haves and the haves nots.

A local television reporter had the camera on Cal and the blonde and began asking them a few questions. Dart tried to edge in as close as possible to catch the conversation. She didn't want Cal to see her. Although on the other hand, it wouldn't matter much if he did.

"I have here with me Mr. Cal Lombard, a local businessman, and his daughter Kelly. Mr. Lombard, how do you feel about your win today?"

The plastic smile was in place and Cal responded lightly "We're just ecstatic, really pleased."

"They're saying that Goombay Smash's win will probably be the history making race of the Maryland Million. What do you think?'

Again the plastic smile. "I think it couldn't have happened to a nicer horse."

This was followed by tinkling laughter all round.

"Well, Mr. Lombard. Congratulations to you and your daughter."

They both smiled and nodded in response. At that point the champagne was being sprayed up in the air. Cal and Kelly made their way with the rest of the winners out of the circle with triumphant expressions on their faces.

Dart didn't know what to make of the scene. She did, however, know that she had a winning ticket to turn in. As she turned away from the winner's circle, she heard a voice call out: "Miss Hastings!"

She reeled around. It was Cal, summoning her out from the crowd. The guy didn't miss a trick. "So nice you could make it," he said his eyes twinkling.

"Oh," Dart stuttered a bit. "Yeah, great race...congratulations."

She noted that his daughter was no longer by his side. Cal leaned closer to Dart and said: "I understand you've been spending time with a Detective Marino." Shaking his head, he continued. "I'd advise against that."

"Oh really?"

His blues eyes were piercing with intensity. "Really. He's not the kind of man you should be keeping company with. Now, on another note, any luck finding out anything about Lester's death?"

"No. No one around the neighborhood has a clue."

"That's a shame." Cal put on a frown. "Well, I'm on my way. The celebration you know. Thanks again for coming down today, Dart." With that Cal was carried off into the crowd.

Dart shook her head a couple times having no idea about the point of the conversation. She only knew that what was said wasn't what was meant—for either party.

Chapter Twenty-nine

The big chest of drawers painted a buttercup gold color had taken up a permanent slot in her landlord's garage shed. It was there to nag at the corners of Dart's brain when she needed it to. Chipping away down through the layers of paint provided therapy. She had already worked down to the first layer on the top of the chest. The first paint treatment was a tan color decorated to look like graining. As she worked on the wood, Dart thought about how the buttercup color had really not given any indication of what was underneath. Really, it was a lot like that with human nature. Sometimes, the first coat was not at all similar to what was underneath at the core.

A strange profile had developed on one Miss Ivy Walker. Dart had always thought she had a real good sense of who the woman was. Now she wasn't so sure. Was she A)the kindly manager of Citylanes B)the prima donna of yesteryear (according to Mabel) C)a woman with a past and a secret or D) all of the above?

All of the constants in this scenario were shifting. Another case in point. Bobby and Billy, two light-hearted jokesters, having a good time. Now they had become, Bobby, a drunk moron, and Billy, a man in the shadows, showing up at odd places and times.

Who else?

That morning's paper had featured in the local section a sizeable spread on Orv Haskins. It gave his whole life story complete with details of his volunteer efforts as a Big Brother---sponsoring fifteen kids over the course of many years. A relative must have written the obit given the slant towards glowing praise. No mention of any gambling interests....Dart's suspect was that he and Lester had a passion in common: the track. The question was how did Orv fit into the puzzle? And why was he killed? Too coincidental to be unrelated that much was sure.

Lester and Orv. Just two regular guys who liked duckpin bowling, a few drinks here and there and betting on the ponies. Dart found it hard to connect that she had physically seen both the men right shortly before their murders.

Her research on duckpin bowling had come to a screeching halt with the murder of Orv. It was almost becoming too morbid of a subject matter to pursue in light of recent events. The title of any research she pulled together would have to be: "Breaking the Duckpin Circle of Gambling and Deceit." She didn't want that.

The crinkling of leaves signaled that someone was making the way through the tiny passageway that led to the rowhouse backyard and the garage shed. Dart grabbed a rag to wipe her hands off as Viola carefully made her way over.

"There you are! I've been trying for an hour to get ahold of you. Finally decided to get in the car and see what's going on."

"Sorry," Dart gestured to the chest. "I've been putting this off too long."

"Watch the fumes, honey, when you're using that stripper stuff. Anyways, I got a call from Eulie Banks, you know, from canasta. Well, she knows folks at the hospital. One of the volunteers was given the job of tracking down no other than Miss Dorothy Hastings."

Dart gave her mother a confused look. "Why?"

"Give me a chance. There's a lady in there, Mabel somebody, she's in the hospital not doing so great. Wants to talk to you as soon as you can get over there."

"Couldn't somebody have just called me direct?"

"You know how the old gal's network is. Rusty at best but always in use. They prefer using the backdoor whenever possible." Her mother fluffed up her hair which Dart noticed was a slightly different tint of ash blonde than when Dart had last seen her.

Wiping down the chest quickly, Dart said: "I guess I better get over there." And in response to her mother's plaintive look, "You can come along."

The hospital sat on a back channel of the city's harbor. On one side of the building, the "patrons" or "inmates", whichever the case, were offered a view of the muck and debris that filled the back channel and eventually pushed along the shoreline. In the horizon, the smoke stacks and other industrial appendages could be made out. If whatever they were in for didn't kill them, the scenic views just might.

Finding Mabel's room number from the desk clerk, Dart and Viola took the elevator up with a child in a wheelchair and her parent. Seeing a child sick and confined had to be one of the worse things going, Dart thought to herself. For once, her mother was silent and had put a lid on her chit-chat. As the elevator made its slow rise to the top floors, the little girl looked up at her mother and said softly, "Do I have to stay here a long time again?" In response, the mother grabbed her hand and squeezed it tightly.

Finally, the elevator doors opened onto Mabel's floor. Viola wiped a tear from her eye as they walked down the hall. "That was a real tear jerker wasn't it hon?" In Viola's world everything had the potential of being a made-for-TV movie. But this time Dart had felt it as well.

They had purchased a bouquet of flowers at the hospital gift store remembering at the last moment not to come up empty handed. Knocking lightly on Mabel's door, a nurse was almost instantaneously at their side. "She's in and out. Here, let me take those for you."

Dart said: "Uh, apparently she's been asking for me. I'm Dart, Dorothy Hastings."

Viola chirped in the background: "And I'm Viola her mother."

"Oh yes, well let me see if I can rouse her."

"Well if she's in pain..."

The nurse didn't hear Dart's afterthought and they could hear a mumbled exchange inside the room.

Dart was briefly reminded of her visit to Ocean City and the similar procedures that had taken place there. She hoped Mabel had not become anything like Mrs. Garrity. She couldn't handle too many scenes like that.

The nurse gestured her in but stopped Viola as she tried to walk in also. "I'm sorry. She just asked for Dart." Viola, with a pout on her face, told Dart that she would wait in the lobby.

The room had the heavy cloying smells common to hospitals. It was dark except for a small bedside light. As Dart approached the bed, she saw that Mabel had shrunk ten-fold since Dart had last seen her a week or so earlier. Her green eyes seemed dulled. She attempted a weak smile when she looked at Dart. Dart felt her heart give a leap. It was definitely a tear jerker day.

Mabel reached her hand out for Dart's which Dart grabbed and held. She felt a faint pulse of life still flowing through Mabel's veins---only faint.

Clearing her throat slowly, Mabel began. "I didn't expect to end up here so soon. I knew there'd come a day.....they always said if I got a bad flu....well, anyway I need your help, Dart."

Mabel explained to Dart in between sips of water from a straw with Dart's assistance that she was making a large bequest to the National Duckpin Congress. She didn't really understand the legal particulars but her lawyer had set it all up as she had specified.

Pausing, Mabel squeezed her hand and then said, "Dart, I've named you the executrix of the endowment."

Dart sat back, stunned. "I don't know what to say..."

"I know it's a big responsibility but you seem to have the spunk that's needed to get duckpin bowling back in its rightful place. You can bring it back, I know you can."

Dart was overwhelmed by Mabel's confidence in her. Or was it just a last ditch stand of a dying woman to save the sport she loved?

Mabel was waiting for Dart's response so Dart said the only thing she could say: "I'd be honored."

"Good, that will make me breathe a little easier. Now, there's something else I need you do. I'd like you to go to my house and get my scrapbook collection. You know where they are---remember?" Dart nodded. "Well, something's nagging me about that day we were looking at them. I'm hoping I'll remember when I look through them..."

Mabel gave her a key and explained how to enter through the back door. After making the arrangements, she looked up at Dart and said: "You should probably do it soon."

Dart understood her meaning and said: "I'll be back no later than tomorrow."

Collecting Viola from the waiting room, Dart felt a weight of depression bringing her down. Her mother was practically tripping over her asking what happened. She didn't know if she was up for the challenge of being duckpin's Joan of Arc but at this point it was a done deal.

Chapter Thirty

Arriving at the bar after 11:00 on a Friday night was a surefire way to be a drink or two down. That's the position Dart found herself in as the buzz and hum of happy drunks filled her ears. But she was perfectly content to have a party for one-----she was eager to catch up and downed her first draft quickly.

A voice bellowed to her on the other side of the bar. Dart looked up to see a couple of fellows from the league.

"Hey girl, how come you didn't sign up yet? See what happens when you live out in the county? You become one of those county snobs." The man could be referring to either Baltimore or Anne Arundel counties. The two surrounding counties were most popular among South Baltimoreons seeking the good life.

Dart quipped back in reply: "Hey, I thought I'd give you a break from my scorecard---but if you're asking for it...?"

She got a half-hearted laugh in return. The league had only finished up a couple of weeks ago and already she was getting rusty. Jokey banter was the glue that characterized playing in the duckpin league. The murders were making her un-glued---that was the problem.

Staring off into space, she realized she was sitting directly in front of that photograph of the winner's of that horse race. The one that had made Lou pledge his undying love for racing. The one that had led him eventually to open this place.

Something about the photo had always nagged at her. What was it? She stared intently trying to figure it out. From the foggy corners of her mind it hit her straight on. She had always recognized Lou as the guy holding the reins of the horse. Up until now, she hadn't known two others out of the four: a young Cal Lombard and a young Al Garrity. Chugging the last of her beer, she headed out of Ivanhoe's.

Dart made a quick turn into the local 24 hour market: Pete's Sanitary Market. She had wondered about this term for a grocery store. Why did they have to label it "sanitary" as if there would naturally be some doubt to its cleanliness?

Grabbing a cart, she attempted to make a quick run through the store for some staples including Romaine lettuce if the wrath of El Nino had abated some. Her cart soon filled up with little Debbies, a head of iceburg lettuce and some soda. As she was circling the corner of an aisle, she heard raised tones. Bobby stood at the end of the aisle. It was clear from his stance and the affronted expression on the clerk's face that he was drunk again.

Dart caught the tail end of the discussion: clear out was the message Bobby was receiving. He lurched away and Dart reflected on how much he had changed of late. He looked about 20 years older, unkempt and, well, like a drunk.

That night Dart slept as though drugged. Her dreams, however, were filled with wild imaginings. When she woke, she remembered in particular one dream sequence involving her and Bobby wandering through somebody's lettuce patch. The lettuce patch was growing abundantly and contained a wide range of varieties. As she trailed behind Bobby, careful not to step on the individual plants, she kept her eyes peeled for romaine---no such luck---it was all iceburg. In the dream she was babbling to Bobby about El Nino and felt desperation about the romaine situation.

The following day Dart managed to get up to Mabel's house much later than she had planned. She parked the car in front of Mabel's house and made her way to the back door. As Mabel had carefully explained, she used the key to the back door. On Mabel's back doorsteps there were two ceramic gnomes to greet her. At one time, they had been brightly painted; now, they were chipped and faded. Otherwise, the place was empty. She shivered to herself, remembering the last time she had entered a deserted seeming building.

Gulping some deep breaths, she entered Mabel Hedges house. Everything was as if she had just stepped out the door. Some breakfast dishes were on the table---a flowered plate and a teacup and saucer. She must have had a proper breakfast before she called the hospital---maybe her last.....

In the front living room, an afghan was carelessly draped across the chair and a crossword puzzle from the newspaper was folded on the table with a pen lying across it.

Dart walked over to the bookshelves. Oddly, it didn't seem like as many scrapbooks were piled up there as before. She took another look before pulling them down. She was convinced: there are been more the other time. Maybe Mabel had taken them into the bedroom.

The condition of the bedroom was even more unnerving. The bed covers were still pulled back. And the wheelchair was in the corner of the room, empty.

Dart made a quick survey. Since Mabel wasn't one for clutter it was an easy job to scope out the room for scrapbooks of which there were none.

Back in the living room, Dart grabbed the four that she had found on the bookshelves and made her way out. Locking up behind her, she walked out onto the back stoop. She could have sworn there were two gnomes; now there was only one.

This was too much. Shaking her head, she walked into the yard and looked around. Nothing. She made a mental note to start getting more sleep.

It was an overcast cheerless day and she was glad to be on her way. She headed straight to the hospital with the scrapbooks. Walking directly to Mabel's floor, she passed the nurse who had been there before. "Oh hi," she said to stop the nurse.

The nurse looked at her questionedly.

"I'm back to see Mabel Hedges."

A look of concern passed over the nurse's face. "Oh I'm sorry you didn't hear--- she passed on this morning."

Dart felt rage surge through her. Mabel had asked her to do one simple thing and she hadn't accomplished it.

The nurse was staring at her repeating the question, "Are you okay?", twice.

Dart sighed heavily. "Yeah, it's just...there was something she wanted me to do for her before she..."

"You know, now I recognize you—you visited the other day. Last night, Ms. Hedges was very agitated and she asked me for a pen and paper. She spent most of the night writing a letter for you. Come with me to the nurse's station. I left it there last night."

At the nurse's station, the nurse looked through the disorganized pile on the desk. Shuffling papers she said: "I know I set it right down here in this pile....it doesn't appear to be here anymore."

Dart, seething over the sight of "the pile system", said between clenched teeth: "These were a dying woman's last words to me. Do you understand that?"

The nurse shook her head and said "I'm sorry. It's got to be around here somewhere. Look---I'll get an all out search going for it and call you the minute..." Dart had already stalked off. The nurse calling after her, "Wait miss I need your number...."

Chapter Thirty-one

Dart left the hospital and drove aimlessly. Eventually, she was in Citylanes neighborhood. She parked the car and began to walk to the market. Looking to cross the street, she noticed Bobby and Dennys Smith of all people at the corner. Dennys in his usual expressive way was using lots of hand gestures. Bobby stood in an angry stance. The two men appeared to be arguing.

Without thinking twice about it, Dart hid behind the nearest available cover, a Tastee Cake truck, painted a baby blue color and decorated with a roly poly tastee cake man that ringed the truck. The truck's rear end butted into an alley which gave Dart a perfect vantage point to watch the men in action.

What could Bobby and Dennys possibly have to argue about?
Finally Dennys threw up his arms and turned on heel. Bobby shook his head and walked down the street. Dart decided to go for it. Keeping a safe distance behind, she began to pursue Bobby. With Marino's warnings niggling at the back of her brain, she headed out.

She saw Bobby get into a car down the street. She quickly hoofed it back to her car and turned it down a side street to catch up with his. Bobby drove an old beater that made keeping him within view easy enough. It was pretty hard to miss a mauve Chevy with big rust blobs and squealing brakes. His driving was erratic and he darted in and out of cars with the practice of a race car driver. Dart felt the sweat form on her upper lip as her own driving took on some devilish antics to keep up with Bobby.

Half of her kept reminding herself that this was a fool's errand while the other half spurred her on—maybe from her anger over Mabel's dying on her. There were too many loose ends, dangling pieces and miscellaneous twists to it all. She wanted answers. After finding Orv's body, she had become intricately bound in the web, as bound as Bobby or Billy or Miss Ivy. And she felt the tightening of that web even while she didn't understand it.

Bobby had finally maneuvered his way out of the maze of city streets and hit the highway. Driving now on the open road he kept a steady clip of about 85 miles an hour---again pushing the envelope from Dart's normally conservative driving habits. She pressed pedal to the metal.

They were headed north on the interstate and she had no idea where he might be headed. For all she knew maybe he was just in a mood for a drive to the country. She hoped, for her sake, that his quest was more purposeful than that.

Twenty minutes later, Bobby still held tight in the left lane cruising at high speeds. Dart, hands clenched on the wheel, was hoping against hope that a state trooper didn't nab her. Suddenly, Bobby's Chevy bolted across three lanes to the right hand turn exit. Dart jerked her wheel narrowly missing a sideswipe with a sports utility vehicle which honked loudly and angrily.

She was on the exit ramp before she even had a chance to register where they were going. As she pieced the interstate exits together quickly in her mind, she realized that they were headed into the county north of the city.

They soon hit traffic lights and she managed to keep a couple cars back from Bobby at all of them. She was close enough however to see him run a hand through his hair in an agitated manner and other expressive body language. Bobby was definitely nervous, anxious, restless or all of the above.

A couple miles down the road Bobby again took an abrupt right into a parking lot. It was the glitzy Double T Diner, a Baltimore area classic. The outside was boldly adorned with shiny chrome and all colors of neon lights. A sign on top of the building showed two big T's entwined in a circle. The place wanted to be noticed. Everybody knew the Double T: from the high school kids who could hang out there all night before they became legal and could move on to drinking establishments to the salesman who could skulk in the middle of the afternoon and while a few billable hours over a piece of apple pie and coffee. For the past ten years or so, the diner had been taken over by a Greek family empire. They had jacked up prices, added baklava and gyros and otherwise ran a tight operation.

Dart edged to the other side of the parking lot to avoid Bobby seeing her. She drummed her fingers on the wheel and contemplated her next move. She would have to sneak in and try for a back booth out of sight.

She waited a few more minutes to ensure that Bobby would already be situated when she went in. Walking along the side of the building she kept her head down. In the entrance foyer she had a good view through the glass plate doors of the interior. "Aha, she thought. She had spotted Bobby at the end of the counter. He was alone. She walked in and asked the hostess to place her in a booth at the far end of the restaurant. It would give her a view of Bobby but he would be unlikely to spot her even if he gazed over the crowd. There were too many people.

Once in the booth she slouched and had the menu up to her face. She was starting to get the hang of this stuff. Her heart was still pounding a mile a minute though and her face was still sweaty. Watching Bobby even from afar she could see that his body language still conveyed distraction. He was not

108

happy. Maybe he just wanted to get away for a bit after his discussion with Dennys. It could be as simple as that Dart thought with a sinking feeling.

"What'll you have hon?" Dart looked up into a heavily mascaraed face crinkled with age.

Softly, she replied; "Uh, just a softboiled egg and some tea. Oh and some toast to go with it."

"Speak up will ya? It's not a church in here you know."

A few guffaws came from some of the surrounding booths. One guy even piped in: "You can say that again. This ain't no church---not with these prices anyways."

Dart cringed inwardly. The woman was going to draw attention to this direction. She kept the menu up close to her face and repeated her order.

The waitress grunted and then shook her head as she walked off.

Dart snuck a look up to the counter and then breathed a sigh of relief. Bobby was apparently oblivious. At this point he seemed to be staring morosely into his coffee cup.

Several minutes went by and Dart tried to stay as focused on Bobby as possible. She almost jumped out of her booth when she saw the lithe figure walk into the room and strode down to the counter toward Bobby. He had on his usual natty attire of tweed and this time also sported an Irish cap---she liked to call them shenanigan hats. It was Cal Lombard himself. This was getting more interesting by the moment. First a heated discussion with Dennys Smith on the street and now an apparent assignation with Cal Lombard at the Double T. Neither one of these men were friendly with Bobby---they just clearly didn't travel in the same circles. What business could he possibly have with them?

Dart watched as Cal took a seat on a counter stool barely looking at Bobby as he sat down. Bobby immediately starting jabbering at Cal, gesturing angrily. Cal in turn calmly placed an order with the counter waitress.

Once Cal had a coffee in hand, he calmly turned to Bobby and said something that quieted him down. He continued to talk, seemingly nonchalant from Dart's vantage point, sipping coffee in between. Eventually, he placed his coffee mug on the counter and removed what appeared to be a checkbook from the pocket of his tweed jacket. He slowly and deliberately penned out a check and handed it to Bobby. Bobby, in turn, snatched the check from Cal and stuffed it in his pocket.

"Okay, here we go." Dart inwardly shouted with annoyance at the waitress. Did she have to be so loud?

"Yeah, thanks." Dart replied back in soft tones.

"Everything okay? You need anything else?"

"I'm fine really."

"Hon, I don't mean to be rude but you got a problem with your voice or something. You need to speak up, you know?"

Oh my God Dart thought I don't believe this woman. She glared at her willing her to walk away. Finally the woman shrugged and walked off. She had been blocking Dart's view the entire time.

By the time she left Dart looked up and nearly shouted out. Both Bobby and Cal were gone, only their coffee cups left behind.

Chapter Thirty-two

On the drive back to the city, Dart debated herself as to whether she should call Marino and tell him about her little adventure. And about Bobby apparently being on Cal's payroll.

Marino had unquestionably ordered her not to continue her involvement in the situation. At this point, Dart didn't know what would be worse: facing Marino's probable anger or not revealing this meeting between Bobby and Cal. Especially since there had been a financial exchange of some sort.

She turned it over in her head several times before finally deciding—--with a little help from the Catholic school girl perched on her shoulder--- that she would indeed have to confess to Marino. Sister Perpetua would be proud.

At home, she checked her messages. Coincidentally there was one from Marino. Terse and to the point, he asked her to call him as soon as she picked up the message. Geez could he have figured out what she had been doing? Feeling sheepish, she placed the call and felt the butterflies in her stomach. Here goes she told herself.

Marino's voice came on the line. "Yeah?"

"Marino, it's Dart. I just got in."

"Good. Listen we got a break in the case and you need to be aware of a few things. Meet me at that coffeehouse you like so much---twenty minutes." He hung up before Dart could respond.

Indignant, she thought to herself, he didn't even know that she deserved the arrogant treatment at this point.

When Dart entered Ruth's House of Coffee half hour later, Marino was waiting for her at one of the back tables. The rest of the place was empty---not surprising for late afternoon.

Marino was sipping on a frothy cappucino and reading the local rag. When Dart walked up, he slapped the paper and said: "They got quite the liberal slant here." He was being sarcastic. "The Liberty" was known for its arch conservative views that almost harkened back to the Stone Age or at least to the era where women should stay close to the hearth and minorities should know their place.

"Yeah, that's the neighborhood for you," Dart replied.

"Can I interest you in a coffee? I don't think they have your swill of choice here."

"No, no. I'm fine. What's going on, Marino?"

Marino sat back and placed his hands behind his hand. "Well, here's how it is Dart. I wanna level with you about this because I think you have a right to know." He paused and then leaned forward and said, "Bobby is going to be charged with the murder of Lester Holmes."

Dart gasped and then said: "Based on what?"

"His lies and a motive. Also, based on a tip that appears pretty solid."

"Where did you get a tip?"

"Well, remember that little nest egg you had set your sights on?"

"Somebody cashed in on Cal's reward money?"

Marino nodded.

"Who?" Dart asked. Marino shrugged. "Great, you mean you can't tell me that."

"It's need to know information."

"Well, I need to know!"

"Some would argue that point."

Dart was quickly tiring of the verbal sparring. Her mind whirled in motion. Who gave the tip that nailed Bobby? It would probably be all over Ivanhoe's soon enough.

"Alright, how do they know the tip is valid?"

Marino explained that the tip had given enough information which led to irrefutable evidence. At least in the eyes of the District Attorney.

"This seems like a witchhunt to me."

Marino stirred the cappucino remaining in his cup with a distracted air.

What Marino didn't tell Dart about was his battles with the assistant DA to not go down this road and his attempts at getting more time to find the probable murderer. City politics were best discussed at another time. The heat was on to nab a suspect and Bobby was the best they had. It wasn't 100% just but then a lot of his work wasn't 100% just. Marino's higher ups were pressing him. They needed a arrest. Too many homicides in the city were drifting out unsolved. The duckpin murder had not occurred at a good time politically. And now there was a second duckpin murder.

Marino would give them an arrest. It may not be all that right on but he was sure that it would shake things up.

"The reason I wanted to tell you this is that pinning this thing on Bobby may do one of two things. It may shake the tree and disclose the murderer to be someone else. What I mean by that is that if another guy is out there he may get rattled about not getting the attention for this thing----and try something else." He stared at Dart as if to judge whether she understood his meaning or not.

"I think I get it---you're telling me to watch my ass in the near future. Alright--- and what's the other thing that might happen?"

"Oh—it might have the reverse effect and the perp won't do anything. If there is a perp that isn't Bobby."

"Come on Marino. You and I both know that Bobby didn't do this. He's wrapped up in it somehow---that's clear---but he didn't do it."

Marino raised his eyebrows. "What do you know lately?"

Dart gulped. She then filled Marino in about the scenes that morning on the street near the bank and at the Double T.

After she finished, Marino looked down into his now empty coffee mug. As the silence lengthened, Dart grew more nervous. Finally she exploded: "Look, I'm in this thing now as much as Bobby or anybody else. I have a right to know what's going on and if I see an opportunity to find out something I'm going to take it."

Marino stood up and threw some dollar bills on the table. He looked at her and said: "I can't stop you from doing that. But I can warn you once again: If you're going to play with matches you're gonna get burned." He sauntered off.

Dart, thoroughly incensed, called after him. "Nice last line Marino. Must feel real good to get that in." Marino didn't lose a beat and continued walking out of the shop.

Marino had set up to meet a rookie detective in front of Citylanes. After a quick jaunt from the coffee shop to Citylanes, they found Bobby Blaze in the alley with a broom in his hand.

The rookie read him his miranda rights. Bobby stood there and shook his head. After Marino finished Bobby said "This just isn't right, you know that this just isn't right."

Miss Ivy leaned against her office door with a stony expression on her face. The rookie cuffed him and the three men began walking out. Bobby turned around and said to Miss Ivy: "See if Lou knows any good lawyers." She nodded in response.

Arresting Bobby Blaze was just a smoking out device, a way to buy time. Stir some things up. After placing him in holding, Marino sat back to wait.

A couple of hours later Miss Ivy wandered into the unit. Eyes darting around she finally spotted him. He stood and gestured to her to have a seat. She fiddled with her hands a bit before finally saying: "It didn't happen that night the way I told you before."

"Okay, why don't you tell me how it did happen?"

She wet her lips and spoke. "While Billy and I was closing up, Lester came back to the alley banging on the doors to get in. We let him in....he was drunk, real drunk." She paused and had a disgusted expression on her face.

"Why did he come back?"

"He wanted his money---his share of the pot. He had left before it was given out. So I gave him his money then he just went on a rampage and said that I was cheating him and all this. I tried to calm him down and that really set him off. He made a move like he was going to hit me. Billy grabbed him and he...fell down."

"Then what happened?"

"Billy helped him up and took him outside. When he came back he said Lester had calmed down and was walking down to Ivanhoe's."

"Miss Walker, how do you think this information helps Bobby out?"

Her eyes darted around. "I...I don't know." She sat back in the chair and sighed. "I just felt I have to do something."

"Well what's the truth then?"

"The truth is what I just told you."

"But you have no idea about Bobby's whereabouts that night?"

"He was with his ladyfriend just like he told ya."

"That's just it. He wasn't with his lady friend that night."

"She's talkin' trash. That's all that is."

Marino didn't think the conversation between him and Miss Ivy was benefiting either one of them. He helped her out of the chair and to the door without any protest from her.

Sitting back down he tapped out a drum beat on the desk. Miss Ivy's revised version of the night of Lester's murder was not too enlightening. But it did raise some interesting questions. He sauntered over to the box to talk to Bobby.

Bobby was a bundle of nerves and, judging from the overflowing ashtray, the cigarettes the rookie had given him hadn't been much help. He looked up with a start when Marino walked in.

"Jesus Christ, do I have to sit here for the rest of my life," he exploded.

"Nah, you could get time off for good behavior." Marino replied.

Taking off his jacket, he took a seat across from Bobby at the table.

"So let's talk about Rita." Rita was the dish that Bobby claimed to have been with the night of Lester's murder.

Bobby squirmed. "Yeah, what about her?"

"Rita doesn't know where the hell you were that night. Her words exactly."

"Look, Marino," Bobby leaned forward, "The deal is that Rita's not all there in the head but...you saw the body on her."

"Bobby, Bobby...we got a problem here. You got no alibi for the night of Lester's murder, plain and simple. Now what can I do but let you sit here some more and think about it."

By the time Dart got down to the bar, there was a large crowd hovered around the center of the room. Dart walked up and said to the crowd in general: "What's up?"

Shirl leaned over towards her. "Somebody finally cashed in on that reward money, that's what's up." As Dart had suspected, the news was out.

Lou passed a draft over to Dart and the story unfolded. Apparently, Wallie, Lester's teammate, had fingered Bobby as having something to do with the murder. Whatever information he had given to Cal and Dennys had been enough for the cops.

Lou talked about how Miss Ivy had come running into the bar desperate for the name of Lou's attorney. He had never seen her so riled up.

Bobby was now in holding. Word had it that he was really cracking up in there. Lou leaned forward and said to Dart in a low voice: "It's probably being cut off from the booze."

Dart left the crowd at Ivanhoe's and headed home. She needed some space to sort out all the nonsense. How did Wallie figure into the equation? Could it be that he was in cahoots with Cal---another one on the payroll? And wasn't Marino smart enough to see through a scam like that?

After allowing Bobby some more simmering time, Marino went back in the box.

"Alright Bobby. Tell you what---we'll forget Rita for right now. How about that?"

Bobby stared at him waiting for the next punch.

Leaning forward breathing into Bobby's face, Marino then said: "What I really want to know about is why are you on Cal Lombard's payroll?"

116

Bobby was not forthcoming with any response. He didn't even appear shaken by the question. His earlier display of nerves seemed to be over. This worried Marino---he had been counting on Bobby getting more nervous.

Coolly, Bobby took his time before countering with: "You know, Marino I've been sitting here thinking. I got rights don't I? I've watched enough cops and robbers shows to know I got rights. You may think I'm a dumb piece of white trash from South Baltimore but I know you're just a wop a-hole from Little Italy. So let me tell you I got rights."

Marino leaned back and sighed heavily. "Your rights aren't looking too good right now. I know these things. So what's Cal been paying you for uh?'

Bobby remained remarkably unphased. "A friendly exchange among friends. Nothing wrong with that"

"Oh the judge might have another opinion of that….."

"You know Marino I've got an extreme case of been there done that. If there's one thing that the Army taught me, it was always watch for what's ahead, you know what I'm saying to you?"

Marino didn't know what Bobby was saying to him but he did know that his strategy was failing him. Remaining poker-faced himself, he mulled over the facts: Bobby was right. He did have rights and these rights were being trodded upon. Wallie's so called "information" was no more than a bunch of contrived crap that Cal had paid him to say. Marino had sniffed that out the second Wallie had slunked into the office---having to repeat his story after he had already supposedly met with Cal and Dennys about the whole thing. Marino, at the time, however, had thought the whole thing might be a brilliant smoking out opportunity with Bobby.

No harm in letting Bobby sit around a bit longer---maybe the nerves would come back. It was getting late though……he was getting hungry.

Chapter Thirty-three

Dart dragged herself out of her car weighted down with some shopping bags from the Sanitary Market (once again, the search for Romaine went on to no avail.) It had been a long night at Ivanhoe's---all the discussion regarding Wallie's betrayal of Bobby had gone on and on. She was getting worn down she thought to herself. As she walked up the stairs to her apartment, she had fleeting visions of the "good old days" when all she had going on was a few business calls and the steady presence of Marvin.

She had forgotten to leave her outside porch light on before she had left. All was dark as she unlocked the door and walked into the foyer. She called out for Marvin. A couple steps in and she felt the bag in her left hand brush against something and then a noise.

Flipping on the light, she looked down. It was a duckpin that she had knocked down. It was spinning on the parquet floor and the overhead light reflected off of it. Before she had time to fully register the situation, Marvin, who must have been laying in wait, pounced onto the duckpin as if it were prey. With that, Dart screamed a blood curdling cry that caused Marvin to skulk quickly out of the room.

Mentally slapping herself Dart told herself to get it together. First order of business was to make a quick tour of the apartment. Nothing appeared to be out of place. She checked the door and windows and they too were intact. No sign of forced entry at least to her novice eye.

Reluctantly she decided to call Marino---just to ask for his advice. She paged him and received a call back momentarily.

After explaining what happened, he said he would be right over and a police cruiser would be there within two minutes. He cut off Dart's protestations tersely: "I tried to make it clear to you what we're dealing with here. You have to start taking this seriously."

As her stomach jumped with nerves, Dart watched out the window. She was glad Marino had called in for the cop but didn't want him to know that. As promised a squad car pulled up momentarily. A heavy set man in uniform got out of the car hiking up his pants as he walked to the door.

Dart opened the door for him. He did the same sort of search that Dart had done and emerged from the back room asking Dart if anything was out of place. "No, nothing," she replied, "Just this duckpin on the floor."

A rapid knock was being tapped out on the door. Marino. Dart thought to herself. The policeman opened the door and let him in. Marino directed all of his conversation to the officer not even looking at Dart. He seemed more than angry. "What did you find?"

"Nothing out of place, no sign of break-in. Only thing noted is the tenpin."

Dart jumped in. "Where are you from officer?"

Perplexed he answered: "Chicago. Why?"

"Ah that explains it." Pointing at the duckpin she said: "Duckpin, not tenpin."

He continued to look confused as Marino grabbed Dart's arm and took her into the other room.

"Hey," she protested.

"We have to have a chat," he said.

He proceeded to explain to her that she should find another place to stay for the next couple of days. They didn't quite know what they were dealing with here.

Marino waited while Dart dodged around her apartment, throwing items in an overnight bag and stuffing Marvin in the cat carrier under much protest.

They parted at their cars outside her apartment—Marino with a worried, absentminded air about him and Dart with a dazed and confused look.

Dart showed up on Viola's doorstep and was greeted with the usual effusiveness exclamations which nearly turned into shrieks as she explained her predicament.

"That's it! We're packing that place up tomorrow and you're moving in with me permanent."

As her mother rambled on about how "nice and safe" her neighborhood was, Dart felt shivers up and down her spine. She didn't know what fate was worse: moving in "permanent" with Viola or facing the duckpin demon head-on by going back to her apartment. In the meantime, Marvin strolled around the kitchen contentedly sniffing for tuna.

By the time Viola and Dart got up from the kitchen table and headed to bed, it was late. Even so, Dart spent a restless evening tossing and turning in the single monk-like bed that was in Viola's guest bedroom. As the night wore on, the apartment was beginning to look more and more appealing, threats notwithstanding.

Marino had pulled a long night. After seeing Dart safely on her way, he had scurried back to the station. His department chief had grabbed him the second he stepped through the office.

"Marino that's enough with the Blaze character. We got nothing on him. Let him go---for the night."

As Marino had feared, in his absence, Bobby had been making noise. Enough for word to get back to the chief.

"Alright, alright chief. I was just trying to get him talking."

"The last thing we need is to hear it from downstairs. Remember that." The imposing hulk of the man that was the chief lumbered away.

Marino had to contend with Bobby's snotty attitude, complete with jeers and wisecracks. Letting him back on the street hadn't felt too good---but couldn't be helped.

Too wired to go home, Marino left the stationhouse and went to Chew and Chat, a local all night eatery. Staring down into a plate of greasy fried eggs and slimy sausage, he could almost make out a duckpin. It was then he realized that the case was starting to get the better of him. Too many long nights with few results.

Chapter Thirty-four

The morning broke clear and warm. More reminiscent of mid-summer than spring. Dart felt the humidity as she rose from bed. Two days with Viola had been two days too many. It had started with the incessant questioning about Dart's old boyfriend, Leo, complete with possible analyses of why the break up had occurred and continued to be a forty-eight hour talk frenzy.

Dart had reached saturation point mid-day the first day. Boiling point had come later and ended with Viola weepy and playing the guilt card. Change was in the air: Dart was left with only one avenue. Over english muffins and hard boiled eggs, her mother suggested again they pack up the apartment. Putting her head in both hands, Dart looked up and said: "This is crazy. I'm going back to my apartment and dealing with whatever this is. Marino can probably put somebody on watch."

Pulling up to the apartment, Dart couldn't help but feel that she was returning to the scene of a crime---which, she thought. was actually the case. It had been a crime committed and she was the victim. And that pissed her off.

She could feel the anger burning in her as she made her way into the apartment. "Come out come out wherever you are" she said, half hoping someone would be there to face her wrath.

Of course, all was still and silent when she opened the door. Just as she had left it.

After unpacking and letting Marvin loose, she decided to get down to work. Into writing half a case file, she looked down and saw her message light blinking.

"Miss Hastings I hope this is you and that I've tracked you down. I'm calling from Harbor General. I found the letter Mabel Hedges wrote to you. It's here for you when you want to pick it up."

Dart called back and got the nurse on the phone. Her first question was how the woman had gotten her number. (Dart had remembered immediately her rudeness at the hospital in not responding to the woman's request for her phone number.) Once again, the canasta connection had worked in her favor and she had tracked Dart down by asking around at the gift shop among the volunteer "blue-coat" ladies. Dart arranged to go to the hospital and pick up the letter immediately. She was too excited by the prospect of what the letter might hold to delay pick up.

At the hospital, she brushed away the apologies of the nurse with her eyes on the prize. Letter in hand, she headed to the coffee shop to read it with a mug of java next to her. It was the little thrills keeping her going these days.

Twenty minutes later, she was seated in a deserted corner of Ruth's House of Coffee holding a steaming mug. She examined the letter in front of her on the table. It had been sealed shut and on the front in a delicate hand her name had been spelled: Dorothy Hastings.

Heart beating rapidly, Dart finally plunged in and ripped it open. It consisted of one page, with writing on one side. Mabel's writing style was not as flowery as her speech. The letter was short and succinct:

Dorothy:

I am writing this to you as I know my time is limited.
I remembered what it was in the scrapbooks. Seeing Al Garrity's clippings reminded me of it because Cal Lombard was in the background.

Here is my message to you: Cal Lombard is not to be trusted. Beware of his murky blue eyes---they hold secrets that we don't need to know.

Sincerely,

Mabel Hedges

Dart groaned in disappointment. "That's it?" she asked herself. "I could have told Mabel that myself."

She reread the letter and tried to think it through. Now at least there was some Al and Cal thread. What could they have had in common? She ruminated some more before turning her attention back to her coffee. She felt that there was some link tying everything together that was within her grasp...she just wasn't grasping it.

She needed to spend some time looking over Mabel's scrapbooks again—she had jammed them in her closet after Mabel had died. Maybe there was some connection in there that she had overlooked. She made a mental note to herself to do so.

Chapter Thirty-five

Climbing the steps of the Baltimore Museum of Art, Dart had a Suzanne Vega song, "Blood makes noise", running through her brain. She had seen too much blood lately, that's the only thing she could figure.

The museum was a monumental structure placed in a treed area in the northern quadrant of the city. It was known in particular for the Cone Collection which consisted of a fair number of Matisse works. The Cone sisters were wealthy eccentric art collectors who had soireed about with the likes of Gertrude Stein and others.

Dart didn't visit as much as she should. She had good reason to swing by today however. She had scheduled a interview with another duckpin great---one of the last on the list. Harry Dingle was a docent during the afternoon at the museum. He had asked Dart to meet him on his break. He had been odd on the phone and very peculiar about when they could meet. Dart chalked it up possibly to the all the recent problems within their little Baltimore duckpin sphere. She was hoping he was more personable face to face.

Walking into the café attached to the museum, she checked her watch. Five minutes early, she wandered over to a table and made herself comfortable. Removing pen and pad, she began to organize questions in her head to ask Harry Dingle.

All of a sudden, there was a low voice at the table saying: "Young lady, are you waiting for me?" Jolted, she looked up and saw a diminutive older man who was bald as a billiard ball. He was dressed in an elegant ensemble more suited for evening than daytime (as far as Dart's limited fashion knowledge could comprehend).

"Harry?" she asked in response.

"That's me." He took a seat in one of the nouveau-molded chairs next to Dart. Looking around nervously, he said "I really don't want anyone to overhear us. I have a reputation to uphold."

Perplexed, Dart said "I don't understand."

Harry proceeded to tell Dart in low tones about his "important" association with the Museum and how he wouldn't want people to get the wrong ideas.

Dart caught on pretty quickly. Harry was an art snob. He apparently viewed his duckpin roots as a source of embarrassment. As Harry prattled on about his connections and other topics, Dart thought to herself: "This guy is a real contrast to the rest of the duckpin crowd." She had assumed that the inherent pride that she, along with others such as Park Canby and Orv Haskins, felt for the sport transcended to all. She couldn't suppress the immediate distaste that she had developed for Harry Dingle.

She made it known to him by interrupting him and saying: "Harry, I'm here to talk about your duckpin days----I'm really not interested in the rest to be blunt."

Harry was taken aback. Once her cut had its affect, he appeared to almost sniff in the air like Myra's French poodle.

Clearing his throat, he redirected the conversation: "Well, what is it you want to know?"

"How did you get started in the sport for openers?"

"When you grew up in a Baltimore neighborhood, it was kind of hard to avoid quite frankly." Harry began to relax a bit. "It got folks out of the house, a way to meet people, make friends, whatever."

"From what I gather, you ranked pretty high for awhile there?"

Looking down at the table, Harry replied: "Yes, I did have my moments I guess you could say."

"Any stories about others you bowled with?"

Harry shifted in his chair. "Like who?"

"Well I kind of need you to tell me. I don't have a complete roster of who was around then."

Harry suddenly leaned forward and hissed: "If this is your way of getting me to talk about Cal Lombard, I simply won't be pushed into it."

Dart felt complete confusion. "Cal Lombard?"

"That's it young lady. I'm sure you can find your way out." Harry stood up and stormed out of the café.

124

Chapter Thirty-six

It was nearly 10:00 P.M. when Dart's phone rang.

"Dart that you?" The raspy sounds of Shirl's voice came through the line complete with background noise of talking and music.

"Let me guess," Dart replied, "You're at Ivanhoe's."

"How'd you...you're one smart cookie girl, don't let nobody tell you different."

"What's up Shirl?"

"You ought to get down here if you can. Bobby got released from the po-lice and boy is he on his high horses. Getting drunker than a coot and going on and on. It's a real show."

After hanging up with Shirl, Dart slipped on some leggings and a T-shirt and headed down to the bar.

She spotted Shirl at the end of the bar and made her way over. On her way, she realized that Bobby was actually standing on a table reading from what sounded like the Declaration of Independence. Lou was glowering from behind the bar and Dart could see it was only a question of seconds before Bobby finally got his.

A small crowd had gathered around Bobby; some jeering, some applauding. It gave him all the encouragement he needed to keep reading aloud. "...right to free speech, right to...." Pointing emphatically at the document he slurred, "See...it says it right here. That cop has no right..."

All of a sudden, Billy Blazes slinked into the bar and made his way over to Bobby. Dart watched as Billy crept up behind Bobby who was oblivious to his brother's presence. Within a nanosecond, Billy had jumped on the table and grabbed Bobby in a front lock, immobilizing him and the table.

The group of people gathered around gave a collective gasp and backed up. Bobby struggled as much as he was able while Billy commandeered him down from the table and then dragged him outdoors.

Lou shook his head then began wiping down the bar as if to punctuate the end of Bobby's little scene.

Dart asked him: "What was all that about Lou?"

"That dumb cop let him out. Boy, he made a mistake there."

"Why do you say that?"

"The guy's a mess. The only place he deserves to be is the slammer." With that, Lou wiped a bead of sweat off his forehead.

The brothers had certainly hit on tough times. A short time ago, they were whooping it up at Citylanes and now…. Seeing Billy manhandle Bobby out of Ivanhoe's had disturbed Dart. She guessed somebody needed to do it…but his own brother treating him that way? He was so rough on him it seemed to her. Or maybe that was just her "girl" response to the situation.

She thought back to a conversation that she and Bobby had had in the alley one night while the League was in session. They had been talking about just things in general and it had led to Bobby's time in Army as an enlisted private. Billy too had also enlisted. They were both stationed in Vietnam at different times. Dart remembered how Bobby had gotten an odd look on his face and had confided: "Hit Billy harder than me." Dart hadn't pressed him for details at the time. She kind of wished now that she had. After witnessing Bobby lately, one would conjecture he had taken in his time in the military harder.

When Dart left the bar, there was a light mist coming down. By the time she headed home, the city had long shut down. The streets were empty. Sighing heavily, she unlocked her car door and began the drive home. It wasn't until she had been driving for a couple minutes and had made a turn at a stop light that she realized something was wrong. There was something rolling around the back floor.

Though Dart could admittedly let things go around the house, she was known among her friends and family as being meticulous with all things related to her car. She cleaned it out religiously. Whatever was rolling around on the back floor had not been placed there by her. Her heart started to pound so she could hear it in her ears. Blood makes noise. Fear crept up her throat. She finally reached a well-lit convenience store parking lot and pulled over under a streetlight.

Getting out of the car she pushed the front seat up and looked. The street light partially illuminated a duckpin. Shaking, Dart reached down and picked it up. A close-up look revealed what appeared to be blood stains on the duckpin. Dart threw it out of the car.

The clerk in the convenience store was staring out into the lot at Dart---suspicious of her activities probably in this neighborhood early in the morning.

She gave herself a shake. She was letting the perpetrator get the better of her. That had to stop. She reached into the glove compartment for a hand towel and picked the pin up. There was no sense dealing with this tonight. It could wait until the morning. She sped off into the night with the clerk still nervously looking on.

Another sleepless night made Dart unprepared for the sun streaming into her window early in the morning. Rolling out of bed, she felt hungover---more from lack of sleep than from too many National's in her estimation. Some might argue.

After a quick cup of coffee and a shower, she headed down to the station house, checking the back seats of her car before getting in. She had left the duckpin on the back seat the night before, wrapped in the towel. She hadn't wanted it in the house. In the bright of the day, it did look like blood on the duckpin.

She managed to get "rock-star" parking right in front of the police station and hurried in, eager to unload herself of the stained duckpin.

As she approached his desk, Marino looked up. A hooded look on his face indicated he had had another rough night as well.

"'Morning," Dart said tersely. She then placed the toweled package on his desk. "I found this in the back of my car last night."

Standing up, Marino opened up the towel. "Well, what do we have here?" he said. Pulling out a pair of rubber gloves from his top drawer, he put them on and then held the duckpin up for inspection. "Looks like it was used to mess somebody up....." He stared at Dart, duckpin in hand.

"Don't look at me," she said hands up, "I'm just the innocent bystander finding planted duckpins here and there." Her voice quivered on the last part of the sentence and Marino could sense she was more upset than upon first notice.

Eyes avoiding the duckpin, she looked at Marino plaintively. "What's going on, Marino? I just want out of this whole mess."

Sitting back down, he put gloved fingertips together. Finally, he said: "I don't know...I honestly don't know."

Both of them then turned to the duckpin and stared. Dart got a confused look on her face.

"Wait a minute," she exclaimed, "I swear that's the same duckpin that was on Miss Ivy's desk!"

"What are you talking about?"

Dart explained to Marino that she had been in Miss Ivy's office after Lester's body had been found, making phonecalls for Miss Ivy who was too upset at the time. Miss Ivy had a vintage duckpin on her desk that Dart had picked up and fiddled with while she was making the calls. Miss Ivy had always claimed that she had won the duckpin in her glory days and that it was one of the duckpins from the original duckpin alley on Howard Street.

Dart finished by saying: "It really looks like the same duckpin---although at that time it didn't have muddy colored stains on it, of course."

Marino leaned forward. "Alright, I'm going to send this over to the lab. Get it tested for whatever's on it. After that, I'm going to take a trip over to Citylanes. In the meantime, you lay low. Understand me?"

Dart nodded. She had a plan of her own in mind.

Chapter Thirty-seven

Once back at her apartment, Dart made a beeline for the phone. Trying the Baltimore Museum of Art, she found out that Harry Dingle wasn't working until the weekend. Explaining she was a family member that had misplaced his unlisted number and needed to consult with him about a sick great-aunt, she easily coaxed the number out of the gentle voiced docent who had answered the phone.

Dialing the number, Dart waited until a woman's voice answered on the fifth ring. "Dingle residence."

"Oh hello I'm trying to reach Harry Dingle?"

"He's not available right now."

"Well do you know where I might find him? It's....urgent."

"I'm really not at liberty to say."

Dart felt like she was facing a stone wall. She tried another tack. "Are you his wife?"

"Oh no, no." Hesitation and then the woman said: "I'm Mr. Dingle's housekeeper."

"Oh right, he speaks very highly of you." Dart lied glibly. "He told me if I ever had a problem contacting him to just ask you."

"He did?" The housekeeper was clearly taken aback.

"Oh yeah, he said he'd trust you with his life. So if you could just give me some idea...I know he's not at the museum today."

"Well, I guess there's no harm...this time of day he's usually already at the Maryland Club."

Dart smiled with satisfaction. "Thank you, thank you very much."

The Maryland Club was one of the hang-outs for Baltimore upper crust society. Where the 'haves' enjoyed rubbing elbows in rooms filled with rich mahogany woodwork and expensive wall coverings and sipped expensive brandy with one another.

Dart decided that she was definitely going to have to dress a part to get the doors opened for her.

Rummaging through her closet, Dart threw out a couple of selections to include a chic black linen dress, albeit ten years out of fashion, and a silk white pantsuit---both courtesy of Viola's attempts to get Dart to dress "more feminine". As the lack of wear attested, these attempts along with others had failed.

The black linen won and Dart added some clunky strapped sandals to finish off the ensemble. She appraised herself in the mirror. Her curly red hair spilled over onto the black dress covering freckled shoulders. The heels of the sandals added a couple of inches to her already towering height. All in all, she looked not one iota blue blood. Sighing, she thought to herself "It will have to do".

The drive into the center of the city was quick and traffic free since it was mid-afternoon. She hoped to get out of there in time to avoid the rush hour---but she'd have to play it by ear. The club was housed in a grand stone edifice dating from the turn of the century. It had taken on all the trappings of the late Victorian period such as an ornate cornice and heavy molded trim around the windows and main entrance. The door handles were weighty brass and shined to perfection. The Maryland Club was hanging on to traditions of a bygone era.

Entering the foyer, Dart was immediately greeted by a maitre de. Speaking in soft tones, he asked how he could be of assistance. Raising herself to her full height, she spoke imperiously: "I'm meeting Harry Dingle."

The maitre 'de replied: "Of course. Please follow me." Leading Dart through a hallway carpeted with a rich Persian rug which made Dart feel like she was sinking, they approached an open doorway. The room beyond was clearly "the men's room". Like Haussner's restaurant, it had the reputation of trying to uphold the men only patron rule for as long as possible. Even if it wasn't legal anymore, tradition hold strong as Dart noted the conspicuous absence of any of her gender.

Several men looked up when she walked in with the maitre de in a bored kind of way. Then ignored her right away. Must be an unspoken response to "female in the room" she thought to herself. They weaved through the room ending up at a table tucked away in a corner where Harry Dingle sat. His attire was understated as compared to his outfit at the museum. The pale blue smoking jacket and dark slacks were nonetheless appropriate for a "men's room".

The maitre de swept his arm and presented her to Harry: "Mr. Dingle? Your guest?" he said with a questioning lilt to his voice.

Harry looked between Dart and the maitre de with bleary eyes. "Yes that's right," he said slurring his words. Dart sighed with relief. Harry had no problem vouching for her maybe because of all the drinks in his system.

Harry gestured for her to take a seat. "'Cuse me if I don't get up. I'm feeling a little...tired. Oh—what would you like to drink?" This was definitely a kinder, gentler Harry Dingle than the one at the museum. She asked what he was having. He replied a gin and tonic. Dart said that would be fine. Gesturing to the bartender, Harry held up two fingers.

On a section of the wall behind Harry, Dart noticed there was some sort of "hall of honor": a series of photographs with tasteful brass plates underneath indicating gentlemen of the club who had distinguished themselves in some way or another. Sweeping her gaze quickly over the photographs, Dart zeroed in on one in particular; a large prominent place for a photo of Cal Lombard. This would be her conversation bait for later on.

After taking a long, slow drag off a lit cigarette, Harry turned to Dart and said: "What can I help you with, Ms. Hastings?"

Dart sat back and began. "Well to be honest Harry I felt that our interview was cut short the other day. I thought maybe we could start over. I don't know if I said something to offend you..."

Harry cut her short. "No, no...you weren't offensive. I'm just a little....sensitive I guess you could say about the 'good ole days'." With that, he gave a small snort.

Dart leaned forward. "Are you saying they weren't that great after all?"

With a far away look to his eyes, Harry didn't speak for a minute. He opened his mouth to say something and at that moment the drinks were brought to the table.

He changed course and lifted his glass. "To the great sport of duckpin bowling, Ms. Hastings."

Dart replied with raised glass: "Always."

The gin and tonic was perfection. Just the right amount of gin (Tanqueray no doubt) to tonic, not overiced. Dart savored the taste by taking small sips. She noticed Harry, on the other hand, was downing the entire drink in one long gulp.

After finishing his drink, Harry began to ramble on with reminiscences of his duckpin days, not unlike the way Park Canby had waxed nostalgic. Dart began to take notes. She would pick through the stuff later---now it was important to get it all done. Especially if he came up with any quotes. Harry was turning out to be much more pleasant drunk than sober.

As he became more wound up, he slipped into the use of a Baltimorese accent, more Hamilton than Guilford. So his duckpin roots did shine through after all, Dart thought to herself, as she watched Harry gesticulate with hands his enthusiasm over a certain tournament.

Finally it was time. She waited until there was a pause in Harry's monologue and then said: "I notice Cal Lombard's photo behind you. He seems to really be a big cheese around town. What did he do to get that dubious honor?"

Smacking his lips, Harry looked directly at Dart. He then said tersely: "Cal Lombard is a bastard." With that he snapped his fingers for another drink.

Dart shifted in her seat. "Well I know he has some charitable associations..."

Harry cut her off. "Yeah, he's real important all right. He's so important that...." He stopped.

"What Harry," she verbally nudged.

Sighing deeply, Harry gazed at Dart with sad eyes. "At one time, Cal was one of my best friends on earth. Al Garrity was my other best friend. I wouldn't have been able to envision a life without either one of them. I lost Al 40 years ago. I lost Cal at the same time."

Dart waited, afraid to break the trust.

Harry didn't let her down. "You see, Cal did something so unforgivable. Something that ruined us all. He is a man without a conscience and nobody knew until it was too late."

More riddles for Dart to solve. But this time she would get more to go on. "Too late?" she prodded.

Harry's eyes suddenly grew big--- Dart felt a hand on her back and a voice say "Too late for what Harry?" She reeled around. Cal Lombard was looking down on her. His hold on her back increased in pressure.

Taking a deep gulp but not missing a beat, she responded: "Too late for Harry to get back into duckpin bowling. I'm trying to convince him it's never too late."

"Admirable, quite admirable," Cal's blue eyes were like flint. He didn't believe her for a second. She rose up jerking his hand off in the process. "Well, gentlemen, it's time I'm on my way." Turning to Harry who was now practically cowering in his chair she said: "Thanks for the drink, Harry." He waved his hand weakly either in dismissal or in goodbye.

She felt the stares of both men on her back as she walked out of the club room.

Walking down the street to her parked car, Dart felt sorry for the wrath that Harry was clearly going to be facing. But why did Cal control Harry too? What happened back in the 'good old days' that had set up Harry in this situation? She cursed the fact that her and Harry's conversation had been cut to the quick. He had really seemed on the verge of divulging all. Did she dare approach him again? Or was Cal now in the process of making sure another conversation between the two of them never happened?

Chapter Thirty-eight

Later that afternoon, Dart got a call from Dennys Smith. He wanted to meet her and made it sound urgent. She agreed; in part, because she wanted a distraction and in part because she had the funny feeling that today's episode with Harry Dingle was going to be addressed. Dennys was integrally wrapped up in Cal Lombard's affairs. She remembered too well Dennys' angry conversation with Bobby Blaze on the sidewalk. Meeting him at his office seemed the easiest solution although he had offered to come to her house.

Dart had also recalled why the distinctive whine to Dennys' voice reminded her of something. She realized that this visit might give her reason to bring it up.

The National Duckpin Bowling Congress, responsible for all the leagues throughout the Northeast, was housed in a dingy overused alley on the southeast end of town. They had been "lent" a corner of the building and it wasn't much despite the airs that Dennys put on. There was just Dennys and a secretary who was cleaning her keyboard with q-tips when Dart walked in. She waved Dart in. They apparently didn't stand on formalities.

Dennys was gazing at his computer and stirred as he heard Dart come in. Bleary-eyed, he offered her a chair and then said: "I'd offer you a coffee but it's not much..."

Dart put her hand up. "Don't worry about it. But you look like you could use some."

"That bad, uh?" Dennys smiled ruefully rubbing his hand over some razor stubble. Dart had finally figured out what was odd about Dennys' razor stubble: it had a layer of pancake make-up on top of it. It made her skin itch just looking at it.

Dart stared at him and waited for him to start. He continued to rub his face and not say anything. Finally she said: "What's up Dennys?"

He took a big yawn and followed it by saying, "This is hard..."

Looking at her watch, Dart said: "Look I've got some other things..."

"Okay, okay..." he blurted out, "Cal and the League want you to lay off Lester's and Orv's murders. They've given the reward money and the case is as good as solved in their minds."

Dart sat back in the chair. "Are you threatening me?" she asked.

Dennys leaned forward and lowered his voice: "Look honey don't get in Cal's way. He's a powerful man..."

"And?"

"Just don't get in his way."

"You know what Dennys...I don't get it. You're supposed to be running a duckpin association. Who do you work for anyway? The leagues or Cal Lombard?"

Dennys shrugged nonchalantly then said: "You gotta keep people happy in this business, Dart."

"I think you need to worry about crossing over the line." Dart could see the anger in Dennys' eyes but she pressed on. "For example, why would you be responsible for giving Bobby Blaze a hard time?"

"What are you talking about? I seldom talk to Blaze."

"Well you certainly were talking to him last week near the market."

Dennys pressed his lips together.

"It's a small town Dennys. And you know what? It gets smaller every day. I finally realized what it is about you: Miss Perkins' P.E. class, seventh grade. Do you remember it---Denise?" In Dart's recollection, Denise had been a very masculine girl, relentlessly teased and unhappy. Although they had not really hung out in the same crowd, Dart had remembered the whine to her voice whenever she had spoken up which had not been often.

Dennys shook his head. "I knew it was just a matter of time before you remembered. Well, so what? I'm a transgender. Big deal."

Dart was in the midst of a huge bluff. She wouldn't use this against Dennys/Denise but he didn't know that.
She remained silent.

Dennys broke the silence. "Look---what do you want?"

"Just get Lombard and company to back off. No more warnings. Got it?"

Dennys said with the whine back in his voice: "Okay, okay. I'll see what I can do. But I am telling you, you really should back off. "

Without waiting for an answer, Dart got up from the chair and waltzed out. She heard Dennys say under his breath, "Shit!".

Chapter Thirty-nine

The lab results had come back and Marino sat his desk puzzling over them. Bobby Blaze's fingerprints were all over the top part of the duckpin. The stains were blood, Type O, but they were still waiting to run further tests. Lester's blood type happened to be Type O. This seemed too pat to Marino. Bobby was being handed over on a silver platter once again. He sighed. He was left no choice but to haul him in and grill him all over again. This game was getting old.

Hearing some commotion near the entrance to the homicide room, Marino looked up. Miss Ivy Walker was storming her way over to him after pushing past the receptionist. Marino groaned inwardly. What now?

Red in the face, he could almost see the puffs of smoke emanating off of her. "What have you done with Bobby?" she screamed at Marino without any preliminary niceties.

"Look Miss Ivy why don't you have a seat...."

"Don't give me any of your sweet talk!" She literally stomped her foot. Marino knew he was witnessing a South Baltimore "hon" in action.

He finally soothed Miss Ivy to the point where he could get a coherent story pieced together. Apparently, Bobby had been missing for a couple days. Miss Ivy had checked all the spots where he might be, including erstwhile girlfriend's houses. To no avail. Bobby hadn't surfaced. Miss Ivy was casting blame on Marino left and right.

"So you tell me Detective. What am I supposed to think seein' as you're one of the last to see him?"

Marino with as much calm as he could muster replied back: "Here's what I'm gonna do...we'll get the word out to our men on the street. A description and places where he's likely to be, okay?"

Slightly mollified, Miss Ivy looked all her years and more as she shuffled out of the station house. Marino felt his blood pressure soar. Where the hell was Bobby? He should have never let him out. Hopefully, it was on a bender and he would surface. If he didn't, Marino had even bigger problems.

Chapter Forty

Mabel's scrapbooks had been stacked in the corner of Dart's closet collecting more dust since her death. Dart finally faced them head-on. She sat down with a tall cold drink and began to pour through the pages chock-filled with newspaper clippings, photographs, and souvenirs.

It was slow going. Mabel had saved every minute detail of her life as a duckpin bowler. In the third scrapbook, Dart turned the page to find the photograph that she had seen at Mabel's house when they had poured through the scrapbooks together---the same photograph that Miss Ivy had underneath her desk: Miss Ivy and Al Garrity holding trophies. She recalled the conversation that she and Mabel had. Mabel's voice came back to her in bits and pieces: "...on that particular day, she [Ivy] insisted that their picture be taken together. What's funny is that after that picture was taken a tradition was started and the top male and top female were always posed together...."

While looking at the photograph, Dart's eyes strayed to the top right corner of the photo. The corner was slightly furled. Frowning, Dart picked at it and discovered it was relatively easy to pry the whole photo up from the page. Turning it over, she saw some faded handwriting. Closer inspection under the lamp allowed her to read it. *Mabel, you could only dream of getting a guy like this. Don't even think about getting in my way.* It was signed: *The Empress!*

The handwriting was basic Catholic school cursive, written by a young hand. Dart had a sinking suspicion that she recognized it: it appeared to be a younger version of Miss Ivy's handwriting which she recalled from the time she used Miss Ivy's Citylanes notebook. Mabel had not told her the whole truth about the picture. She had alluded to Ivy as a problem but that was it. Why would Mabel have saved the photograph when it had such a nasty note on the back of it? Maybe Mabel's saving habits had just provided some valuable insight.

In the following pages of the scrapbook, Dart encountered clippings about Al Garrity and his funeral. As Dart studied a faded newspaper photograph of Al's coffin being carried through the church doors, she realized that several of the pallbearers were familiar faces, minus forty years or so. Examining closely with a magnifying glass, it appeared that Harry Dingle, Cal Lombard and Lou from Ivanhoe's, of all people, along with two unidentified men were the pallbearers.

Dart tried to think this out. Lou had never acknowledged knowing anybody from the duckpin crowd of the 60s. As far as Dart had known he was into horse racing and then running a bar---that was about it. So how did he factor into the equation?

Dart then recalled the photograph hanging behind Ivanhoe's bar. There was something about the photograph that had always tickled the undersides of her brain. And now...she was pretty sure the same cast of pallbearers were also the exact same men in Lou's photograph. It was time for a long-overdue chat with Lou.

It was early afternoon. She could pretty much guarantee that she would have Lou to herself without much distraction. After parking her car, she walked up the street in drizzling rain, determined to get answers and face Lou head on.

"Hey Dart!" Lou greeted her as she walked up to the bar. Beaming a smile at her, he leaned on the bar. "What are you drinking?"

"Make it a 7 and 7, Lou."

Lou lifted an eyebrow. "That's a new one for you but 7 and 7 it is." He turned behind the bar and grabbed a bottle of blended rye whiskey.

They were silent as he prepared the drink. The tinkling of the ice in the glass and the pouring noises were comforting. Dart knew when he handed her the drink she would have to break the silence.

"There you go missy," Lou placed the drink in front of her.

She gulped a big sip and then looked at him watching her. She began: "You know Lou I've always meant to ask you about that photo you have there." She pointed at the framed photograph behind the bar.

Smile still in place Lou replied: "What is it you want to know?"

"Actually I don't think I need to ask you anymore. I think I've already figured it out." She paused for effect. Lou's smile cracked just a little.

A few more seconds passed. Then he said: "'that right?"

"Yeh, I've finally figured out who all the players are. There's a young Cal Lombard, a young Al Garrity, a young Harry Dingle and...then...there's you."

"I have to hand it to you---those research skills are paying off. But...it's no secret who we all are. "

Dart scratched her head. "I don't know, Lou. It just seems funny to me that you didn't mention your connection to those three before."

Lou snorted. "It's no connection. It's just a photo. A photo taken a long time ago. It's up there to remind me of how I got where I am." Dart knew he was referring to the winning money on the horse which allowed him to buy the bar but she played dumb.

"And how did you get where you are?"

"The track. That's it."

"Funny how the track didn't work out so well for Lester and Orv, isn't it? Or do you know why the track didn't work out so well for Lester and Orv?"

"Look, missy. I don't mind answering questions to a point. But now you're messing in areas that are best left alone. I have said all I have to say on the past."

"Lou, two men have been murdered in the name of the past. How many more to go? If you know how this all fits together, you have to speak up. If not to me, then to the police. "

Lou became stone faced. "Awhile back I told you all I can tell you on the subject. I can't help it if that's as far as you can take it."

Dart exploded: "Lou, you told me nothing! You whispered 'Hi-Ho-Pimlico' in my ear. Give me a break."

Lou leaned towards her with menacing bulk. His voice was low. "Look it. I worked damned hard to get what I have. You think I'm going to blow it all over two bit hustlers like Orv and Lester? For the record: I'm not."

Dart backed up. She knew when it was time to let go.

As she collected her belongings, Lou rubbed his forehead and said more to himself than to her: "Sometimes, I wish I had never seen that horse."

Chapter Forty-one

The call came in at 3:30 AM. Marino had drifted off into a sound sleep a couple hours earlier. The persistent ringing of the phone had been intertwined with dreams about Dart throwing duckpins at him; him dodging them as best he could. Then the phone ringing corresponded to getting hit with them. He shook himself free of the dreams and grabbed the phone.

"Marino here."

The caller identified himself as Sergeant Lowery from the stationhouse. "Marino, we got some action down at South District. Caucasian male, mid-30s found bludgeoned to death. Body left in a construction site Jiffy-john. It's been there a while---the construction crew hasn't been on-site for a few days."

"Who found the body?"

"One of those bums that hang out down that part of town."

"Exactly what part of the district are we talking about?"

"Down in the marshes...you know where all the industry is. You can't have industries without marshes for them to dump in, you know what I'm saying?"

Marino knew too well. The environmentalist groups had complained loudly and clearly on the topic.

Marino told the sergeant that he'd meet him down there and began to pull articles of clothing on. He tried to keep from thinking too much until he was more awake but his overriding thought was Bobby Blaze.

By the time Marino made it down to the scene of the crime it was nearly four. Bright lights provided illumination of the scene and several uniformed cops were already milling around with crime tape and other accessories that went along with the aftermath of a murder. It was probably more activity than this side of town had seen at four in the morning in a long time.

They had waited for Marino before removing the body from the Jiffy-John. Smells emanated from the john and Marino braced himself for what was to come. Directing them to open it up, he stepped closer and the horrible odors of death and decay hit him full force. They flashed a high powered flashlight behind him so he could see more clearly. The body was crumpled at the base of the toilet bowl with its head perched on the open ring of the toilet. Dried blood literally coated the head. Nonetheless, Marino could make out the now mottled features of Bobby Blaze. Shaking his head, he stared down at the corpse until the sergeant next to him cleared his throat.

Marino spoke up. "Okay let's get the body out of here and then dust this thing for prints."

The ME had arrived by this time and once the body was laid out on the ground, he confirmed that it appeared to be death by a blow to the head. No one mentioned the obvious: Lester Holmes and Orv Haskins had been dealt the same type of fatal blow.

Chapter Forty-two

The news ripped through the city by daybreak. Some cub reporter looking to make it big time had leaked it out and dubbed it "Another Duckpin Strike". By the time Marino stumbled back to the squad room at 9:30, the phones were ringing off the hook. Calls were primarily from the concerned citizenry of South Baltimore. Marino had a big message on his desk: SEE THE BOSS. Underlined twice.

He was waiting for Marino, fire spitting from his eyes. After launching into a prolonged tirade, the chief wrapped it up by stating: "There will be no serial killer on my watch! Do I make myself clear?"

Marino had slunked back to his desk, head pounding from too little sleep and too little caffeine.

The phone rang insistently and felt like it was right inside his ear. "Yeah," he picked it up and answered tersely.

The reply he got back was just as terse. "So now who do we have as perp?" Dart's voice chirped across the line.

Before Marino could answer, she continued: "...and what about all that stuff about flushing the real perp out? Meanwhile Bobby Blaze was hanging out on a limb this whole time. I mean, he may not have been the most honest guy in the whole world but..."

Marino stopped her. "Forget about it. You're out of the picture. I don't want you involved anymore. I'll figure this thing out. I just need everybody to get off my ass."

On that, he hung up not waiting for any reply.

++++++++++++++

Dart stewed on the other line. Slamming the phone down, she got up and began to pace back and forth. She needed a cigarette. Marvin attempted to pace with her until she accidentally stomped on his tail at which point he meowed and bolted out of the room.

What now? Bobby Blaze was dead. It was getting down to nobody left to kill...although if she could ever figure out the motive she might also know who was left to kill.

All potential information sources were locked up tight. Lou wasn't giving an inch. Miss Ivy was in the middle of it all. Cal Lombard was the bad guy for reasons not completely understood. Harry Dingle probably had his mouth permanently sewn shut since the last time she saw him. Harry Dingle---that's right. Dart remembered she had never followed up with him, longshot though it probably was at this point.

Grabbing the phone she punched out the number listed in her notes.

There was an answer on the first ring. "Yes," a voice whispered.

"Harry, is that you?"

"Oh it's you again. I can't talk to you anymore. I just can't."

"I understand Harry. I understand that Lombard's got some hold over you. Can't you just give me a clue?"

There was silence on the other end.

Dart took it as an opportunity to plunge on. "There's been another man killed Harry? You know that don't you?"

Harry made a noise that sounded like a sob. Then he said: "I know, I don't..." Suddenly, he made an abrupt shift. "Look, meet me in a half hour." He paused and then said; "At the powder magazine at Fort McHenry. You know it?"

Dart replied that she did.

Harry ended the conversation by saying: "We'll talk then."

Dart held the phone away from her ear and stared at it. There had been a dramatic shift in the conversation. He had gone from a weak almost sobbing Harry to a concise on the ball action Harry. "Well...I guess you shouldn't look gifthorses in the mouth," she told herself.

Putting on a light windbreaker, Dart headed out for the Fort. Surrounded by water, the fort was more often windy than not in the spring. And judging from the clouds in the sky, it would be chilly as well. Fort McHenry had served as the primary defense against the British when they had tried to take over Baltimore during the War of 1812. It consisted of a pentagonal shaped complex on a point of land that jutted out into the Patapsco River. Comprised of outer walls and a dry moat, the interior of the complex had been housing quarters, the guardhouse, a powder magazine and officers' quarters.

Dart skipped the visitor center and made for the powder magazine. She knew the Fort like the back of her hand having spent a summer as a volunteer intern back in her earlier years. What the average visitor did not see was the series of tunnels and connecting passageways between the surviving buildings---perfect for Sunday afternoon games of Dungeons and Dragons which she and other volunteers had sometimes engaged in on slow days.

The park usually starting closing up at 5:15 so she assumed that Harry had some connections to allow them to meet there. She had made a point of parking her car outside of the gates just in case---she recalled too well the hassle to get someone to unlock them. When she got into the interior courtyard, there were not any people around. Probably they had all been herded out by the diligent rangers in charge. The powder magazine was located in one of the corners of the complex. A brick structure with ten foot thick walls, if Dart remembered correctly, it was distinctive from all the other structures with its gambrel roof pitch. Walking towards it, she noticed the heavy planked door was slightly ajar. She had assumed Harry would meet her outside the building but maybe he was having a look around.

She opened the door fully and stepped into the windowless barrel vaulted room where powder had been stored 170 years earlier. The light was dim but she spotted something in the corner. Walking closer, she froze in her steps. One of Mabel Hedge's gnomes grinned maniacally at her from its corner position. Stifling a scream, she scurried backwards too late---the door to the magazine slammed shut and Dart was suddenly engulfed in darkness.

Chapter Forty-three

Marino spent the day dodging phone calls and trying to come up with a new game plan. The old one hadn't worked. With Bobby dead, it would become even more dangerous. He was no longer around as a foil for the real killer. The real killer would get nervous.

Then the call came in. The secretary was screening all of his calls unless it was pertinent to the case. In other words, she was weeding out all the nutcases and fruitloops. So far, she had become fairly proficient at it. When his buzzer went off, he picked up the line.

"Marino," he said tersely as ever.

The voice was thin, raspy. "We got her."

"Excuse me?"

"If you want to see Dart Hastings again, you cooperate. Leave South Baltimore boys alone. Look for your killer elsewhere."

Marino felt ice down his spine. He had warned her again and again and now...clicking his fingers he got the attention of a deputy and gestured for him to turn on the tracer at the same time trying to keep the conversation going. "Uh...how do I know this is not bullshit?"

"Now, now," the voice whispered, "You're too smart for that detective. You wouldn't take any chances would you?"

Abruptly the line went down. The deputy shook his head. They hadn't gotten a line.

Dart tried to concentrate on her breathing and make it regular. "Breathe in, breathe out" she told herself over and over again. She had developed claustrophobia as a child and it had increased in severity with age. The darkness was total and complete. As she practiced her breathing techniques, her eyes adjusted more to the surroundings. She found that she could just barely make out the edges of the magazine.

Moving slowly, she reached a hand out to touch the wall. It bumped up against the cool damp of the chalky plaster that covered brick. She felt along the wall until she reached the slight shelf before the wall crawled up to meet the ceiling. She racked her brains to remember if there was any sort of interior exit to the tunnel. At the same time, she felt around the ledge. Nothing. She slumped to floor in disgust. How could she have fallen for this? It was one of the oldest tricks in the book. Luring the unsuspecting victim to an isolated place where no one could find her for hours---maybe even days. No, that wasn't true. The rangers would open the magazine up for the visitors in the morning. But it was going to make for a long night....unless...what if the killer or killers were going to come and get her from this location. Was she to be the next bludgeoning victim?

She scrambled to her feet and tried to search out any openings. Moving slowly, her hands reached out to touch the walls. As she moved along, her feet suddenly bumped against something. Too late, she remembered the gnome. It knocked over and the ceramic shattered—the noise bounced off the magazine's walls. Avoiding the pieces of Mabel Hedge's gnome—which were likely shards ---Dart continued her search. After what seemed like hours but was probably only minutes she gave up again. Time was an odd entity in the dark.

Sitting down on the wood slat floor, pangs of hunger began to set in. She hadn't grabbed anything to eat before heading out the door to the fort. Now she was paying the price....

Her mind started to work overtime and she imagined all the possible scenarios of her "release" from the magazine. None of them ended up favorably. If only she had thought over Harry's suggestion before heading out...oh well...hindsight never helped.

Harry Dingle. Dart had been viewing him as a possible ally---source of information---when actually he had become an agent of malfeasance. His version of the old duckpin crowd had been like all the others: pleasant and benign...until the subject of Cal Lombard had come up. He had certainly painted a dark picture of Cal...

Bits of conversation with Harry came back to Dart: "You see, Cal did something so unforgivable. Something that ruined us all. He is a man without a conscience and nobody knew until it was too late."

And then there was Mabel Hedges skirting around the whole truth about Miss Ivy. All she had recognized was that Miss Ivy was a prima donna but yet there had been a nasty note from Ivy on the back of the photograph of her and Garrity---clearly directed at Mabel.

Lou's reaction when asked about the old crowd had also sidestepped the truth. He had patently refused to answer direct questions about Lombard and Garrity.

Finally, Miss Ivy at Haussner's the night of the dinner with Dennys Smith had flat out not been willing to discuss Garrity at all---ending the conversation by making them leave the restaurant.

Dart didn't understand much of it but what she did know was that there was some sort of ring of protection around Cal Lombard. The old gang, for whatever reasons, was covering for him. Harry had tipped her off at the Maryland Club by babbling some of it in his drunkenness. But he hadn't given away nearly enough. That's why Dart had been so eager to meet him here.

So what had Lester Holmes known or done to Lombard to get himself killed? And Orv Haskins too?

Leaning her head back on the wall, Dart began to slip into a dreamfilled sleep. She found herself in Citylanes bowling on a team with Miss Ivy and Mabel Hedges. They were bowling against Lester, Orv and Billy Blaze. They were all the same age in the dream and shared the same kind of friendly rivalry that Dart had known during her time on the Citylanes league. The dream took a twist when Cal Lombard walked in with a bag of duckpins. In between rolls he would run up a lane and add duckpins to a player's set. The funny thing was that everybody went along with it. Except for Dart---she began protesting to Miss Ivy who told her to shut up. The culminating scene was her protesting once too often and Cal lunging towards her and taking a swing with a duckpin that he pulled out of his bag. She woke before the swing hit its mark.

Startled awake, she forgot her surroundings and felt the panic of claustrophobia set in. She needed light to feel better. She talked herself out of the panic attack and practiced the deep breathing techniques once again. To divert her attention, she thought back about the dream. Funny how the group dynamics in the dream were not that far from real life.

There was something in the dream that tickled at the corners of her brain. Shaking herself, she tried to figure it out. Going back through the dream again, it finally came to her: too much had gone on around the time that Miss Ivy and Al Garrity were champions together. It was the same year that the picture was taken that hung in Lou's bar for example. Also it was the year before Al Garrity was killed. And come to think of it, it was year before Bobby and Billy Blaze were born. She remembered Bobby bragging on time about how he had graduated high school right on time; unlike his brother Billy. Right on time was 1987 meaning they were born in 1969. A pivotal year given all the events that had transpired.

What was the connection between all of it? Lester and maybe Orv too must have known something; something bad about Cal or something else. Was it the parentage of the twins? Miss Ivy was at the bottom of it all. When she got out of here, Dart told herself she was going to make a beeline for Citylanes.

Chapter Forty-four

Marino had sent out a swarm of cop cars in search of Dart. All cruisers had descriptions of her, her car, and even her mother. He was trying like hell to cover all bases.

With all the point men out in the field, he decided to stay in the office in case she called in. He also decided to place a call to Viola.

The line picked up after a couple of rings. Viola answered groggily: "Hello?"

Marino apologized for the late hour and then asked if she had heard from Dart.

Viola's tone sharpened up. "No..why? What's wrong?"

Marino hesitated a second too late. "Well..."

"My God...what's going on? Where is she?" Hysteria kicked in immediately. Marino could have kicked himself. He really bungled this one.

"There's nothing to worry about yet, Mizz Hastings." He went on to explain the probable prank call and explained what he was doing.

Viola went into a sheer panic vocalizing it all to Marino. "What should I do? Oh my god, my baby girl."

Trying to calm her as much as he could, he suggested that the best course of action was to sit by the phone, emphasizing that she shouldn't leave the house.

She began to protest and he had to cut her off by saying "I've got to go but please tell her to call me right away if you hear from her."

A call was coming through from Callahan, one of the beat cops that he had sent out to check Dart's apartment.

Callahan's voice crackled through dispatch. "No suggestion of foul play, Marino. Her car isn't here either."

"Okay, keep on surveillance until I tell you otherwise. Over and out."

Another call was patched through to Marino. One of the lab guys had been pulling some overtime and had made a positive identification of the blood on the duckpin in Dart's car. Not only was it Bobby's fingerprints on the duckpin---

it was also Bobby's blood. It may have been used in the beating of Bobby before he died. And had then been placed in Dart's car.

Marino looked at his watch. One A.M. The waiting would continue.

Dart wondered how many hours had gone by. There was no way to tell. Too bad she hadn't sprung for one of those neon delights the last time she had been wristwatch shopping---there was no way to read her old fashioned Timex.

Her mind began to wander and she thought back to her D&D days. She remembered the Dungeon Master had maps that showed where the tunnels were located. The group usually hung out in the more convenient passageways to play the game. They had always talked about doing an actual staging someday using the entire tunnel and passageway network but they never had. It was around the time where there had been a couple of incidents where kids had been killed playing out the real thing. When it got right down to it, they all chickened out.

Dart had spent a lot of time pouring over the old maps---the maps had fascinated her, revealing a slice of the city that few knew about. It was even suggested on the maps that the tunnels extended from the fort approximately one and one half miles to the South Baltimore neighborhood---where Citylanes was.

Using all powers of concentration available to her, she tried to conjure up the maps in her mind. Had the powder magazine been connected to the other buildings? Then it came to her. No, it had not. In fact, she and a guy in the group had talked about the section of the tunnel that extended to the magazine. It was a dog-leg---almost as though it had been constructed as an afterthought. She had had a crush on this guy and would have followed him anyway. As it was, she had followed into the section of tunnel linking the powder magazine to the visitor center. It was all coming back to her. She hadn't been paying too much attention to her whereabouts but she remembered that he had pointed out where the entrance into the magazine was.

Now—all she had to do was figure it out in the dark. The logical place for the connection was probably somewhere near the entrance opening. Dart crawled along the floor to make her way to that area. Once she found the door---by bumping right into it---she methodically felt around the door for anything out of the ordinary.

Awhile later, she hit paydirt. Pieces of plaster were missing along the walls: there was such a section near the door. Brick was exposed and a brick was slightly out of alignment with the other bricks in the section. Pushing on it in all directions it finally moved. Like a piece in a jigsaw puzzle, once it was removed a couple of others near it were moveable. After four bricks had been removed, Dart felt the wall. Under her hand, there was a wood plank. A door? That was her best guess. Continuing with her work, she removed all the other loose bricks until she had uncovered a door. Where a handle should have been placed there was a hole. Pulling on it with her finger, it gave way to the pressure and pulled back.

Holding her hand out into the space the air felt dank and old. That's right she thought to herself. There had been a rung staircase leading up to the door. Careful not to fall into an open hole, she felt at the base of the door and indeed felt stair rungs. Now she had to make the decision to go down into the tunnel without any light....

Chapter Forty-five

He stood over a worktable. He picked up a navy blue vinyl bowling bag from the floor and removed its items one by one: duckpins. He laid them out in a circular pattern on the workspace in front of him.

Then he pulled out a photograph and a black marker from the drawer below. Marker in hand, he slowly drew a line through the person in the photograph, simulating the symbol for a strike used on scorecards.

Placing the photograph in the middle of the circular arrangement he stood back as if to admire his handiwork. The struck-out face of Dart Hastings peered back at him in the photograph.

Turning away from the table, the killer pulled on a black jacket and headed out.

Chapter Forty-six

Time marched on and Dart sat on the powder magazine floor in a cold sweat. She was scared to death to go down into the hole but also scared to death not to go down into the hole. Meanwhile, more time meant a greater chance that her captors might show.

Finally, she stood up. Zipping her windbreaker as high as possible and pulling her jeans down as far as they went, she attempted as much body coverage as possible. Moving at a snail's pace, she took one rung at a time. After counting five rungs, she reached her foot down and felt it dip into water. She shook it out quickly. She had guessed water might be involved but had not been too excited at the prospect. It had been a dry season those many years ago that she had walked through with her crush. Taking a deep breath, she dipped one foot in again and tentatively felt for bottom. It wasn't too bad---it was wet up to her ankle. She could handle that. The smell was another matter---the water or whatever it was smelled as though it had been stewing for the ages. She tried not to think about it.

On both feet, she put her arms out on either side and felt for the walls. She was rewarded with a cold slimy feel on either side. If memory served, she figured the tunnel was about 2 1/2 feet wide and probably not much higher than her height. She began her journey forward.

It was slow-going. Several hundred yards into it, there was still no light but the water level remained about the same. Then Dart rubbed into something with her leg----something soft and furry that squeaked. She jumped about a foot and splashed water in the process.

"Oh God..." this was the worst yet. A rat. And how many more were there? One of Baltimore's lesser claims to fame was a thriving rat population. In some neighborhoods, they even "fished" for rats with fishing poles as a way to get the attention of public officials. Newsclips of "rat-fishing" didn't help tourism much---the average suburbanite probably didn't rank rat-fishing very high as a sport.

Shivering up and down, Dart swallowed her revulsion and prayed she wouldn't get bit. After wading for about ten minutes, there was a break in the water level and she found herself not standing in water. A welcome relief. Except that as she walked forward she banged into a wall. Exhaustion gripped her--- was this a deadend?

Using her hands she felt around on the walls until she discerned that it was a fork in the road. Big decision---which way to take. She tried to think about what direction the tunnel had headed in. I

It was too disorienting. There was no way to really tell. Left might be the direction of the park entrance---maybe.

She headed that way. After moving forward for what seemed like the better part of an hour, Dart was finally greeted with a pinprick of light in the distance. Choking down sobs of thankfulness, she moved more quickly until the light became brighter and brighter. Finally she was on top of it. It was the outline of a door. Like the door in the powder magazine, it consisted of three heavy planks with two crossboards.

Feeling down towards the doorknob area, she realized there was no doorknob. Nor were there any hinges. She pushed and then pulled on the door---anything to get it to move. It wasn't budging. She began to kick on it with the last bits of energy left to her. If the door was hinged on the other side, kicking it open would be her only shot. She could feel it start to give way. Creaking with complaint, it began to open. Dart then thrust her whole body weight against it. It opened enough for her to squeeze through.

On the other side, she blinked ferociously to adjust to the light. It didn't help that the room was lit by a battery generated spotlight---the kind that clicked on in people's backyards when you weren't supposed to be there. A quick look around reminded her that this room had always been used as storage area--- and a discreet make-out hideaway. It was filled with supply boxes and also costumes shrouded in plastic. Probably the reenactor's club was allowed to store their stuff in the room.

A staircase in the far right corner indicated the exit. Dart leaped for it, eager to get out of tunnels and darkness. She burst through the door at the top of the stairs and faced head-on a security guard sitting at a desk with a very surprised look on his face.

"What the..." he yelped as he dragged his considerable weight to his feet.

"Oh...I didn't expect to see anyone...I've been trapped down there. What time is it?"

"It's four-thirty...what did you say---trapped?" Dart watched an expression of suspicion and disbelief came over his face.

"Yes...really. I don't dress like this for kicks," she added gesturing to her mud-stained clothes and wet shoes. The stench covering her spoke for itself. A nervous giggle bubbled up and spilled over.

Giving her an "okay, I've got a crazy on my hands" look, he said out loud, "Miss...I'm going to have to call the park manager about this. You wait here..." He lumbered off to another room.

Without much thought, Dart leapt towards the main entrance. Lucky for her the doors pressed open from the other side on their own. If whoever was after her, she didn't have time to chat with overweight security guards. She needed to get help and fast.

Running out of the building she headed for the park gates. She squeezed through a small opening next to the gates. She half expected her car to be missing. But it was there. Just like her keys were there in her jeans pocket buried deep down despite rolling around on magazine floors and crawling through water logged tunnels. Her car started right up and she headed out without lights turned on. There was enough moonlight to see her way. Aside from that, she had become pretty proficient at seeing around in the dark. She didn't want to alert anyone out there watching.

In the shadows, the dark figure hung back behind a tree and watched Dart frantically working on her car lock. A grin spread across his face. He watched her finally get in the car and speed off into the night. He laughed out loud when she didn't turn on her lights. She thought she was so slick. His laugh had a tinny noise to it.

Chapter Forty-seven

She headed for her apartment figuring she'd call Marino from there. As she drove out towards the highway she flicked her lights on and stepped on the gas. Talking to herself she laid out the next course of action. After calling Marino they would go...wait a minute if she called Marino she'd be tied up for hours doing all the official crap that he'd probably have to do.

She had to go confront Miss Ivy right away---but by the time Marino finished with whatever it may be too late. When she got to the apartment, Dart had another plan lined up. Prowling around, she searched for signs of break-in before getting into her apartment. All seemed to be in order including a very groggy Marvin who she didn't have time to pet. She grabbed the tape recorder she used for the duckpin interviews and some packaging tape.

Unless she could get words on tape, the killer would continue to roam free. He covered his tracks that well. It was all circumstantial right now. Dart knew enough about this business from watching countless tv detective shows and reading countless more mystery novels. The only proof is in a confession. Miss Ivy knew who it was and she could steer her that way.

She headed back out of the apartment locking it quickly behind her. As she started down the stairs, she jerked to a stop mid-way. A cop in uniform was standing at the bottom of the outside staircase---blocking her way. It was the same barrel-chested cop that had checked out her apartment after the duckpin incident. She tried to remember his name...it was...Callahan. That's right. And he was from Chicago.

He looked up at her with a grimace on his face. "Miss, you know you got a lot of people looking for you right now?"

"I do? How did they...hey look, I got to run an errand but I promise I'll be right back."

"Uh-uh," it came out like a deep grumble in his throat. "You're not going anywhere."

They stared at each other for a couple minutes. Dart figured she could probably dodge around him but was it worth it?

She breathed out some air. "Alright...can you get Marino over here quick?"

In response, he labored up the stairwell, gently nudging her arm to move ahead of him.

Once inside, Callahan picked up the phone and called the station, speaking in acronyms and code numbers.

Dart had plopped down on her sofa, never minding her tunnel stench and stained jeans. The adrenaline kick was wearing off and deep exhaustion was setting in. She knew she had to hold out until Marino got there.

Looking over to the cop she said, "Hey would you mind brewing some coffee? I got some in the freezer."

With a surprised look, he headed into the kitchen and Dart heard his slow movements. Funny she thought to herself, but she hadn't craved a cigarette the whole time until now.

Just as the smell of freshly perked coffee wafted under her nostrils, there was a loud banging on her apartment door.

The cop hustled over and opened it, letting in Marino and a couple of plainsclothed guys.

Dart looked up at the group with bleary eyes. She said: "I think I know who killed Lester Holmes."

Chapter Forty-eight

It took a lot longer than Dart had the energy left to tell her tale from start to finish. Especially with Marino periodically expressing outrage. Finally she got to the part about how she pieced together all of the coincidences.

"So you see," Dart finished up, "...all fingers point to Miss Ivy. As a matter of fact, before Sergeant Callahan so kindly stopped by, I was all set to head out and get what we need." With that she pulled out her hand-held tape recorder and held it out for inspection.

She continued: "So...I still think you should let me go over there and..."

Marino held up a hand for her to stop talking. "Enough, I've heard enough. Let me think this out."

Dart yelled over to Callahan. "How about getting Marino a cup of joe?" Callahan obliged.

Marino absently mindedly took the cup and began to pace Dart's hallway.

The rest of the group sat around and tried not to look at one another.

Finally, he came back over. "Here's this deal. This is totally against my better judgement but I think it's a stab at something. But we're going to do it my way." He gestured towards Dart's recorder. "For starters we're going to rig you up with the real deal."

The phone suddenly rung as if to punctuate Marino's statement. Dart made motions to get up to answer but Marino put a hand up. "Wait," he hissed, "We're setting up a tracer. Act natural when you answer and try to keep them talking as long as you can."

Dart stood up and felt fatigue try to bring her back down. Picking the phone out of its cradle she said "Hel.." and was quickly interrupted by Viola's shrieks of relief which led into a one way monologue of questions and recriminations. Dart looked at Marino and mouthed Viola. He told one of the guys to stop the trace. Dart finally cut her mother off by saying: "I'm exhausted, I'll call you after I get some sleep first thing. Promise." Knowing full well she may not be able to keep that promise---first thing anyway.

The staging of Dart's confrontation with Miss Ivy proceeded uninterrupted by phonecalls or anything else for an hour. Marino made it clear that there was no hard evidence against Miss Ivy and he didn't personally think she had done the job on Lester or on Orv Haskins. However, he did acknowledge that some of Dart's theories may have hit the mark. Although he never came out and said it, Dart figured that Marino was getting desperate for answers and was also viewing Miss Ivy as their only shot.

After laying out the plan, they determined that the place and time would be Citylanes in mid-afternoon---around 2 o'clock. Assuming Miss Ivy was still operating according to her normal schedule. In the meantime Dart was sent to bed to catch a couple of hours of sleep---with the background comfort of Callahan and his crew watching outside. If anyone was trying to get at her, he (or she) had to go through a battalion of Marino's men first.

When she woke, the plainsclothes detectives helped her rig up the tape recorder by taping the wires around her stomach. Chagrinned she looked around her living room at the sea of guys staring at her white stomach being taped up. Marino, talking on the phone, caught her eye and gave her a wink. She stuck out her tongue. It was like a scene from a weird porn flick.

The guys then coached her on how to not give it away that she was wired. Marino came over and sat next to her. "Okay here's the deal. We've had a tail on Miss Ivy for a couple of days. I checked in with the boys and they say she entered Citylanes an hour ago. It's time for you to head over." As Marino said that, Dart felt some nerve ends prickling.

Marino looked at her with a concerned expression. "You're okay to do this, right?"

"Yeah. I'm going to do this." Even though Dart knew she was the bait. The old bait and switch maneuver. Textbook murder solving.

Chapter Forty-nine

Driving to Citylanes Dart steeled herself to face Miss Ivy and get answers. There would be no stonewalling this time like she had pulled at Haussner's that night. In the course of the past couple weeks, Dart had mentally altered her impression of Miss Ivy. Everything from her cold-heartedness about Lester's death, to the collection of duckpin monies, to the odd scene at Haussners had played into her change in sentiment. The sanctioning business had cinched it.

It was humid out and the tape itched. Dart would have to resist scratching.

When she pulled up to the alley all was quiet, typical for a weekday afternoon. Running up the stairs, she strode into a darkened alley keeping taut nerves at bay. Only the office light was on. Miss Ivy was seated at her desk reviewing some account books. She looked up as Dart approached, her skunk streak of white forelock illuminated under the ceiling light, and then calmly closed the books.

"Have a seat Dart. I was expecting you."

Dart stopped in her tracks. "You were?"

"Sure, I knew a smart girl like you, researching like you do every day, would figure things out."

"What exactly did I figure out?" Dart asked.

"How I killed Lester right?" With that, Miss Ivy picked up a duckpin on her desk and tossed it back and forth. She must have replaced her vintage one after she had used it. She stared at Dart with glazed over blue eyes.

"Alright, alright. You want me to tell you the whole story I guess. Really, have a seat and I'll start at the start."

Dart find herself slumping into Miss Ivy's visitor chair too stunned to counter.

"You see, I wasn't smart like you Dart when I was young. I was just a sweet naive girl from South Baltimore who liked to play duckpin bowling. I didn't bother much with boys or clothes. I just liked to bowl."

She sighed deeply and continued. "When Al Garrity gave me a tumble, I didn't know what was going on. You shoulda seen him. He was such a beautiful man---my Prince Charming." She smiled at the memory of Garrity.

"Of course, he was married....but I didn't think he would let that get in the way. After all, it was true love." She snorted in derision.

"But it did get in the way didn't it Miss Ivy?" Dart asked.

Miss Ivy sat back in her chair, duckpin still tossing back and forth. "The night I told him I was pregnant he told me that I should fish or cut bait. Just like that. I knew he wasn't the man he had pretended to be. I convinced him to meet me one more time for old time's sake. I borrowed my mother's Buick and met him in a parking lot up in Parkville. His weakness was the love of the drink. He kept it hidden from most people but I knew. I had got a bottle of Scotch and encouraged him to drink and have some laughs with me. We sat in his car and once he was good and loosened up I hit him hard with a karate chop to his neck right here. I had seen it done in a Cary Grant movie." She pointed to a spot on her neck. "Then, I pushed him over to the passenger's side and drove the car to the top of Taylor Avenue."

"Didn't anybody see you during all of this?"

"There was just one car that drove by and I figured it was just another drunk like Al." As it turned out, it had been another drunk, and his account about seeing someone was discounted based on his poor reputation. Dart remembered reading about this in the old newspaper clippings.

"Anyways, I set Al back in the driver's and then let the car brake go. And the car took off with speed from the hill. I ran back to my car quick and while I was running I heard the car hit the tree. I was long gone before anybody knew better."

She ended with: "He shoulda known better than to treat me like that."

"So...you had the baby. Or was it babies?"

Miss Ivy got a faraway look in her eyes. "They were the prettiest babies you ever saw. Plopped right out one after the other like they were ready to set the world on fire. Twin boys. I could barely believe it."

"Why couldn't you keep them as your own?"Dart asked.

"Are you kidding? I had my bowling career to consider. Don't you realize that I was the top seated female bowler for ten years?" At that moment, Dart looked into the eyes of Miss Ivy and realized she was crazed.

"So...what happened?"

"Well I went up to Buffalo New York to stay with my cousin Esther. I had them up there. I had already set it up with Margie and Jerry Blaze to adopt them. They were in my neighborhood and Margie had let me know they were having problems getting pregnant. Also, they didn't mind me staying close by and spending time with the boys. Actually I was their built-in babysitter."

"So they didn't know they were adopted?"

"Nope. Not until that damn Lester tried to spill the beans."

"Lester found out how?"

"He came here that night after the league championship. He was...owed some money---you probably heard about it." She shifted uncomfortably in her seat. It was the most uncomfortable she had looked throughout the whole discourse. Dart was amazed that out of all of it the off-betting would bother her.

"Well yeah I did hear about the off betting. But I didn't know it was for that much money."

"It weren't. It was just a couple hundred he was owed. But he started pressing me for more. Saying he knew stuff about me and the twins. He was drunk as a coot just like Al got sometimes...." Miss Ivy got a faraway look in her eye.

Dart pressed her for more and said: "But how did Lester know that you were the twin's biological mother?"

Miss Ivy looked at Dart: "Huh? Oh, he found out from Myra. "

Dart was still confused. "How did Myra know?"

"Myra grew up on our block. She babysat for the twins sometimes. One day, she snooped around through Marge's vanity and found the original birth certificate. Except for telling Lester, she kept it to herself, I'll give her that."

All of a sudden, Dart felt a presence behind her and the door clicked shut. Dart reeled around in her chair. It was Billy. He was holding a small shiny derringer.

Miss Ivy gasped. "Billy whaatt....."

"Why don't I pick up the story from here," he said pointing the gun towards Dart.

This was a different Billy, cool and direct with none of the skittishness he usually exhibited. He picked up on Miss Ivy's thread. "I was there listening the whole time Lester was hounding Ivy and when he got to the part about me and Bobby I listened real good. We had always suspected of course. She was more of a Mom to us than Margie Blaze. Miss Ivy went wild on him and struck him with the duckpin that used to be on her desk---from the winning game. He was so drunk anyway that he fell right down. I pretended that I was just coming in when I find the two of them. She explained he had been abusing her for more betting money. I told her not to worry and I would take care of the whole thing. And I did."

"So you killed him and strung him up in Lane 7?"

"Oh no, I just personally delivered him to some of his, shall we say, friends?"

"The track guys."

"That's right. Lester shoulda learned if you're going to play with fire you're going to get burned."

Miss Ivy had been listening attentively. She finally asked Billy, "You...know the truth about me now?"

Billy's eyes softened a little. "I'll keep your secret as long as you want me to. We're the only ones who know about any of this." He then looked towards Dart. "Except for Dart that is."

Dart now knew that the vein of insanity or whatever it was must course through the blood of this family. The gun was still beaded on her. And the look in Billy's eyes had intensified. Dart didn't believe for a minute that Billy had handed Lester over to "track guys".

She thought quickly. "Look I was just checking into all of this for fun. I'll just drop it now. No big deal."

Billy gave a snort. "Fun? You think it's fun to smear my mother's name?" Raw anger began to radiate from him.

Dart continued. "This can end right here. Lester had it coming to him---poetic justice and all that stuff."

Billy grabbed Dart's arm. "Come on."

Dart stared at Miss Ivy. "Miss Ivy, stop this. You can't mean to go along with this."

Miss Ivy had an expression on her face like a deer caught in headlights.

Billy began to drag her from the office and led her up the staircase to the third floor. His nails were digging into Dart's arms. Dart tried to think her way out of this but nothing came to mind. She remembered that she still needed to get a confession from Billy on the tape. Marino and his men would hold off rushing in unless they could hear serious trouble on the line.

She thought to herself I've got to keep him talking. That's what they always say in all those suspense novels. "So Billy…" It was difficult to start a conversation when the other party was dragging you up stairs. "Was there a reason you've been popping up at places where I am…"She suddenly remembered seeing him on the boardwalk at Ocean City. "Like on the boardwalk for example?"

"Lady, I've been watching every move you made. I knew you was hungry for that money. Just like my brother---greedy as a beggar for money." He made a noise of disgust.

At the top of the stairs, he pulled her along to a closet door. Oh Jesus she thought he's going to stuff me in the closet. "Billy please anything but a tight space… I'll freak out. I'm warning you."

Ignoring her, he opened the door and bent down to remove something. Entering into the closet with a firm grip on her she realized he had revealed an opening and they were walking through the closet into another room.

Once in the room she stared open jawed. It was a space about 15 feet by 20 feet. A skylight, clearly original to the construction date of the building, flooded the room with natural light. This allowed Dart to take in some of the sights. A quick look revealed that this was Billy's den of horrors.

The room was decorated from top to bottom with various paraphernalia. One wall seemed to be devoted to Vietnam. The insignias and emblems of the 83rd airborne division stood out as reliefs in cubby holes that had been constructed on the wall along with various pro war bumper stickers. Another wall was filled with photographs of Miss Ivy and himself. Upon closer examination it was evident that Bobby had been cut out of them. There were also numerous newsclippings. One wall was almost bare except for…Dart felt wobbly at the knees at the sight---a blown-up photograph of Dart with a symbol for a strike in the middle.

Part of the floor that Dart stood on was inlaid with glass block with some sort of light source from the bottom. It must have taken Billy years to make the room given the intricate patterns and attention to detail.

Billy had been watching her and seemed satisfied by her reaction. He said:"See what I got going here is a replica of Sir John Soane's Museum. That's a museum in London."

Dart looking around here said: "I..I know. I've been there."

"Oh I get it," Billy said with a sneer, "You're trying to figure how a South Baltimore guy like me would know anything about Sir John Soane's Museum."

"No, really Billy, I wasn't..."

Waving the derringer at her, he squawked: "Shut up and stay put. I'll tell you all about it. Good old uncle Sam was kind enough to provide me with a stop-over in between tours in Afghanistan. That's how I was at the museum."

He continued to ramble on. "So you see? I got culture just like you Mizz Hastings. See how I fixed this place up real good?" Directing his gun towards the glass block floor, he said: "Sir John was a smart man. He made use of light anywheres he could. That's why I rigged up this glass block to let the light in up here and I got a bulb underneath. Thomas Jefferson rigged up the same kind of thing. And over there," he pointed to the corner where two full length mirrors met, "that gives you your illusion of space."

The more Billy talked the more time Dart bought. As he rambled she tried to work out a plan. The plan basically became: get him to talk more about the murders.

She said: "Not to get off the topic, Billy, but does Cal know about this room? He owns the alley right?"

Billy snorted. "Cal. I got him wrapped up tight."

"How do you mean?"

Billy gave her an exasperated look and began speaking to her like she was a small child. "Cal tells me what he wants and I get it done. In return he leaves me alone. I could re-do the whole alley. He wouldn't care."

"What did Cal want?"

In the same ridiculing tone, Billy began listing. "He wanted Lester delivered to the drug guys, he wanted Orv picked off..."

Dart interrupted him. "Why? Why Lester? Why Orv?"

"Because they were in debt and they were becoming liabilities to the business. Weighing Cal down."

"How were they becoming liabilities?"

Billy suddenly reeled in a purple rage on Dart. Reaching out to grab her with his free hand, he dropped it and said: "Lester threatened to tell tales on Cal. Orv knew the same tales Lester did since they was buddies from way back. Those morons thought they could play Cal like a tin whistle." Almost to himself, he said: "They learned."

The story was finally being pieced together in Dart's mind. There was just one bit of missing information: What did Lester and Orv have on Cal Lombard? She decidedly to boldly come straight out and ask Billy. His neuroticism appeared to be back in check.

He looked at her with stone eyes, one blue stone and one green stone. "They just knew stuff," came his dull reply.

Dart changed tack. "So did it take a long time to pull this room together?" she asked as she gazed around striving for non-chalance.

Billy warmed to the subject. "Yeah, all those old newspaper clippings of Miss Ivy. I had to hunt them down in the library and go to her old duckpin bowling pal's houses."

"Like Mabel Hodges?"

Billy affirmed that he had gone to Mabel's and looked through her stuff---while she wasn't at home. That explained the missing clippings that Mabel had recalled on her deathbed to Dart.

"So how did you get into my place with the duckpin?"

Billy sniffed. "That was child's play. I snuck your keys out of your jacket one night during a league game. Went down to Benson's Hardware. He gave me the key to get in while everyone was playing. It told him I needed to make a copy of a key. Which I did."

Dart felt the hair on her neck rise. Why had Billy wanted to get into her place back then? That was before any of the murders had taken place.

In response to her silent question, Billy shrugged and said: "You never know when you might need to get in somewhere." He stared at her with those dead stone eyes.

He added: "And you know when you were at Mabel's? I took one of the gnomes away. So you know how it feels to be played with. Did you notice where it ended up?"

Of course Billy was talking about putting it in the powder magazine at Fort McHenry. Ignoring his gleeful smile, Dart nervously asked another question, a loaded question. "What did go on between Al Garrity and Miss Ivy?"

That got Billy off the topic of gnomes. "Nothing went on! You're just like Lester and Orv making assumptions again. Well you saw what happened to them didn't ya?"

Dart backed up a little from the waving derringer.

"What did they know then?"

"They knew that Miss Ivy was our mother, me and Bobby's. They thought they knew more."

"More like what?" Dart knew she was pushing it but she plodded on.

"More like she killed Al Garrity. She didn't kill him. Cal Lombard just made her think she did."

"So Cal Lombard killed Al Garrity?"

"I didn't say that, did I? I said he rigged up the whole thing so that Miss Ivy got the idea to get Al drunk then push the car." Billy paused with a troubled look on his face. Then he said as if to assure himself more than Dart. "She wouldn't have killed no one. Not Miss Ivy."

Dart perceived the weak link in the armor and decided to go for it. "Well, what if she did kill him? Can't say I blame her much. If a guy dumped me like that... but I guess it is kind of heavy to know that your mother killed your father."

Billy whirled on her and took a couple of menacing steps. "I oughtta..." He stepped back and clenched a fist.

"What Billy? You oughtta what? Kill me like you've killed Lester, Orv and even your own brother, Bobby? What's stopping you? You think this is fun for me---dragging it out. Let's get the show on the road."

Surprise played across Billy's face but then was replaced by an evil grin. "You think you can outsmart me, uh? Just like those damned doctors at Walter Reed after I got back ." Suddenly, Billy grabbed his head with both hands. "Well you can't!" he yelled at Dart, "and they couldn't either. I am in-vin-ci-ble." He dragged out each syllable and then laughed manaically.

Dart quaking with fear inside knew he was on the edge ready to topple. All she needed was a couple of more minutes to get him to confess.

What could she say?

Chapter Fifty

Marino was in a van parked a block from Citylanes. He tapped his fingerboards with a rapid motion on the dashboard. The conversation between Dart and Billy was coming in scratchy. Billy was more of a nutcase than anyone had bargained for. That much was clear. Two techs worked on the radio to ensure they didn't miss any of the conversation.

"Hey Marino you wanna knock it off. You're making me kinda nervous." One of the techs commented to Marino, gesturing towards Marino's tapping figures.

Marino responded: "You're nervous? How do you think she feels?"

The tech shrugged.

Callahan was also in the van. He was chomping on a bagful of Dunkin Donuts. Marino interrupted his feast. "I'm thinking this is getting too hot. We better get ready to go in."

Callahan stopped mid-bite, "Don't think that's a good idea. We've come this far...she'll let us know if she can't go on."

Marino reflected back to the impromptu prep sessions in Dart's living room. They had gone through the drill many times---it included a couple of code words for SOS in case things got to be too much. At the time, however, they had thought that it was only Miss Ivy they had to contend with. Billy was another story. Still, in listening to the conversation occurring in the alley, Dart seemed in control.

Marino leaned forward into the radio waiting for Dart's signal.

Dart studied her fingernails with feigned nonchalance. "You know, I can sort of understand taking out Lester and Orv. They were troublesome and, quite frankly, you had a job to do for Cal. But the one I really don't get is Bobby. I mean, your own twin brother."

Billy started pacing in a circular fashion. "Shut up. Just shut up. You don't know nothing about Bobby."

"Well I know he was becoming the local drunk. I saw him plenty of times at Ivanhoe's making a fool of himself. I know he lied to the cops about where he was the night of Lester's murder. Was he here with you? Did something go down that he wouldn't keep quiet about?"

"I'm warning you...."

Dart took a stab in the dark. "You know I wonder if he walked in on you killing Lester! Yeah that's it. He saw you do it."

"Damn him! Damn him! It's always had to be his way! Well for once it was going down my way. And he just couldn't handle it."

Dart waited. Billy leaned against a table and started talking as if in a trance. "He walked in that night drunk as a coot cuz he lost the stupid game. He sees me stringing Lester up and asks what the hell I'm doing. Scared me. I thought I was the only one around. Then he tried to take Lester down. He was still breathing at that point. Bobby was so drunk he could barely stand much less help Lester down. I knocked him out and then when I finished up the job, half carried Bobby out and took him home."

Dart knew this was it. This was all they needed---if they had gotten it on tape. She gave the signal outloud. "This is duckpin country!" Billy looked at her quizzically. Then he picked up some dark gloves and started pulling them on. Silence filled the room. There was a clock ticking somewhere. Send in the calvary Dart thought to herself. "It's time," he told Dart. He took a couple of steps towards her and she edged backwards. Waiting.

Right on cue, the door to the secret room crashed open. Marino at the helm yelled outloud: "Drop the gun, Blaze" Marino and the swarm of uniforms behind him all had guns drawn.

In Dart's mind everything was blending together. The mirrors created a mélange of images. The reflections of Marino and his men seemed to bounce off several different walls. While Billy loomed large in her foreground.

Billy kept his derringer on Dart. "Anyone makes a move she gets it," he said in a laconic tone. He seemed unaffected by the pressure.

Dart felt her breathing raspy and shallow.

Suddenly a voice filled the room. "Billy. Leave that poor girl alone and drop the gun."

He turned his head slightly to look at Miss Ivy. "Why'd you tell him I was up here? " he asked in a child-like whiny tone.

"Baby I've known about this room the first day you started building it. But you know I've always let you boys have your fun." Holding back a sob, Miss Ivy continued, "The fun's over now."

Marino held up a tape with his free hand: "Billy we got enough on you to send you away to never never land."

Still staring at Dart, Billy let his gun fall to the floor. It clattered onto the glass brick.

Chapter Fifty-one

It wasn't until after Billy had been cuffed and hauled away that Miss Ivy was confronted. Dart sat in a corner of the room that had always been Miss Ivy's domain. This time, the tables were turned and Miss Ivy was no longer in control. Marino positioned himself behind her desk. He interrogated her on exactly what she had known about Billy's activities.

Miss Ivy, tears running down her face, had confessed that she had known Billy was "touched" as she termed it. But she claimed that she never knew he was involved in murder. When Marino questioned her about the secret room she said she had viewed it as "cute like a playroom". Billy had asked her never to go in there and she didn't. As she put it: "I respected my boys' privacy, just like they respected mine." Dart assumed she meant that neither Bobby or Billy had ever quizzed her on her role in their lives.

Which brought Marino to Bobby. Hadn't she finally put two and two together when Bobby was found murdered? Shaking her head in denial Miss Ivy said no. "I mean I knew Billy was a little jealous...but I never..." Convulsive sobs overtook her and she rested her head on the desk.

Finally she looked up bleary eyed. "When I finally realized he killed Bobby was when I saw those pictures on his wall up there." Dart remembered too well the vivid images of Billy and Miss Ivy with the obvious jagged edges of where Bobby had been cut out. Miss Ivy fumbled for a tissue and then blew her noise. Dart and Marino waited. Miss Ivy continued: "When I saw it...I knew. It was him that killed Bobby. And he has to get punished for that...."

Dart was surprised. She had presumed that Miss Ivy would fight any incarceration of Billy----just like she had fought it for Bobby when he had been held.

Miss Ivy then asked in a small voice: "Can I go home now?"

"Just one more question. What was going on with outside betting?"

Miss Ivy choked back another sob. "It was no big deal. You'd think I was a bank robber or something. A small group of us placed some bets on what team would win---that's all. The kitty was up to about a thousand. I kept good track of it. There wasn't any funny business. I was going to pay Lester his money....I swear, but he just made me so darn mad."

Running a hand through disheveled hair, Marino explained to Miss Ivy that she had to go down to the station. Miss Ivy was alone---no Bobby, Billy or even Cal to take care of her. Maybe that was her main problem: she had always been protected.

After Miss Ivy shuffled out of Citylanes, Callahan gestured for Marino and held up a cell phone.

Dart went out to the lanes. One of them was turned on. She took some practice rolls. Hitting 8 pins on her first roll, she grimaced. Her game had gone downhill. The thing that didn't make sense to her about all of it was this: Billy was too smart to get caught in this trap. Unless he had counted on Miss Ivy's protection, or he had wanted to get caught.

Marino walked over and interrupted her musings. "Let's go for a drive. We got some loose ends to tie up."

"What…. now?" Dart asked.

Marino answered: "Come on."

They hopped in a police cruiser, Callahan at the wheel, and headed into the northern half of the city. As they headed north and blew by familiar landmarks of the city such as the World War I monument on Calvert street and the older run-down yet charming office buildings, Marino explained to Dart how he had tracked down Harry Dingle when Dart was resting before going to Citylanes. When confronted, Harry had pleaded his innocence with Marino. He claimed that he hadn't set Dart up on purpose---he had had no choice. Billy, who Harry understood to be one of Cal's lackeys, had been holding him at gunpoint. Billy had anticipated Dart calling Harry back at some point. He had programmed Harry to direct her to Fort McHenry. Harry had assumed it was all under Cal's authority that Billy was acting. At that point, however, Billy had moved closer to the edge. Although Harry had been scared for his own life, it had been him who had called the station house that day to alert Marino.

No one had realized that Billy had been primed and ready to take action regardless of Cal's say in the matter. Harry didn't set Dart up---he had no choice.

Since their talk, Marino made sure Harry Dingle was being watched. That was how Marino knew where Harry was right now. Dart wasn't surprised when they pulled up in front of the Maryland Club.

As they walked into the club, Dart asked Marino: "Does he have any idea we might be joining him?"

Marino snorted and said: "Like he has a choice."

They went through the same routine that Dart had been through. It seemed like light years ago when actually it had only been a couple of days. The maitre de politely escorted them into the Red Room.

Harry was seated alone at a big table eyes glued to the television monitor in the corner. There was an O's game being broadcasted. As they approached, he looked up and gave a start. Then he seemed to relax back down.

"Hello Ms. Hastings, Detective, welcome to my club. Well I like to call it 'my club'---obviously it isn't just mine."

Harry was as peppy as ever despite or maybe because of the smell of martinis on his breath.

"Harry, we need to hammer out a few details." Marino got right to the point.

"I assumed as much," Harry said. He gestured towards the plush leather chairs situated around his table. "Please, please. Have a seat."

An unobtrusive waiter appeared at Harry's side and stood for direction. "Let's have some champagne and oysters on the half shell all around. After all, I understand we have something to celebrate."

Marino and Dart looked at each other in astonishment. How did Harry know what went down at Citylanes? It had been under a couple of hours.

"Let me clear up your confusion. The Baltimore old boy network is alive and well even if we do use such antiquated methods as the telephone. Word spreads where it needs to spread."

The waiter again made an appearance and uncorked a bottle of champagne. The bubbly was poured and passed to each person.

After Harry initiated a toast, he started to talk. "We all knew Ivy and Al were having an affair. We all guessed she killed him." Long pause. "Nobody went forward. I think I can speak for the others in saying that the guilt---albeit varying levels---has been with all of us for thirty seven years. Except, of course, for Cal.

Pausing to guzzle some champagne, he continued: "Cal's a different animal. I realized that too late."

"Ivy was definitely angry enough to kill Al for what he had done to her but she probably wouldn't have done it if Cal hadn't spurred her on. The deal was that if she killed Al then he would protect her. And make no mistake, Cal assisted Miss Ivy in the murder. My suspicion has always been that what Miss Ivy didn't know was that Cal drugged Al before their date. That's why he passed out. Cal's the one that planned it down to the last iota. He knew Ivy was an easy tool for his plan---which, by the way, left no proof of his involvement."

"But it must be said, for whatever it's worth, he has protected her ever since."

Dart certainly knew this to be true. She remembered too well the incident over the league sanctioning.

Harry continued: "And they both kept each other's secrets. He also helped out with the twins. Miss Ivy wanted to be spared the humiliation of pregnancy out of wedlock. Cal helped her set up the adoption which ensured she could have the best of both worlds---she could participate unobtrusively in their upbringing. Also, the Blazes', like most other families in the neighborhood, could always use some extra money. Miss Ivy provided that via Cal. When Citylanes owner was selling, Cal stepped in and bought to ensure Ivy wouldn't lose her job. He has served as her protector all these years."

Harry paused as the waiter set down a glamorous looking tray of plump oysters on the half shell. Harry then gestured towards the tray: "Please, help yourselves."

After dosing one with cocktail sauce and gulping it down, Dart decreed them superb---even though it wasn't a month that ended in an "r" which supposedly was when oysters were at their very best. And the champagne polished it off rather nicely. So this was how the other half lived she thought. She looked over to see Marino finishing one off with equal aplomb.

Harry continued: "The only thing they didn't figure on was a leak. The leak was Al Garrity. He told me a couple of weeks before he was killed that Ivy was pregnant. I, in turn being younger and foolish in my time, blabbed it to some others after a few nips here and there. The result being that when the murder happened we all suspected foul play. But none of us wanted to rock the boat for...." Harry slowed down and then said, "for reasons..." his words trailed off....

Dart asked quietly "Reasons?"

Sighing, Harry said: "Cal had something on all of us."

Dart waited until he continued on his own. "Lou, even though he won big on that horse, had gambling debt up the wazoo. Cal financed the bar for him---encouraging him on the other hand to tell everyone he had come into money at the track. Lou, aside from owing Cal the bar, also wanted to save face and keep his story intact."

"Orv and Lester. Same story. Gambling debt beyond comprehension. They were almost indentured servants of Cal's. Cal bought out Fontana years ago—but allowed Orv to remain in name only. That's why Orv never sold the land and made the killing everyone thought he could make. Lester, bless his grimy heart, worked as a machinist day in and day out. And every penny went to the track and if it didn't go to the track it went to Cal. We already went over Miss Ivy's debt."

"As for me, Cal knows some things about shall we say my habits or maybe we can call them my choice of companions that I preferred didn't get out to a larger society. It seems silly now with gay marriages going on in Hawaii and whatnot. But back then my world would have caved in. I was beholden to Cal Lombard to not tell anyone I was homosexual."

Dart said: "So here's the six million dollar question: Why did Cal want Al dead?"

Harry takes a deep drag off of his freshly lit cigarette. "Why else? Money. It's the only thing that has ever driven that man. Cal got involved in some, shall we say, dubious dealings right at the start of his otherwise promising career. Al stumbled upon Cal's shady side and threatened him. He told him to clean up his act or he would expose him---no matter what cost. To be honest, I've often wondered if Al would have actually done that. You know, he certainly was no saint himself. A Catholic husband and father of five kids running around with a unmarried woman. But back in the day, that kind of stuff was not considered to be of much importance. Look at JFK for God sakes. But your business was another thing altogether. And many, like Al, held themselves and others to a moral tightrope. You also must remember that Al held a high level job at the Army Corps of Engineers---in other words, Al worked for Uncle Sam and did not take this responsibility lightly. "

"So there you have it. A cover-up based on a shaky foundation of trust between so-called friends."

"What made it finally crack-up?" Marino asked.

"Something so incredibly minor. Lester being a poor sport about duckpin bowling. He was so pissed off at the thought of Bobby beating him again that he had to pull that dumb stunt. Who knows? Maybe he was sick to death of being trampled and beat down his whole life."

At this point, Dart picked up the storyline: " So after the whole scene that night of the league game, he still wasn't satisfied with winning. He had to go to Miss Ivy, hound her for money---and then when she didn't have it, he threatened her. He and she go at it. He brought up Garrity's death. Ivy became unraveled probably because it has eaten at her conscience all these years. And then she hit him with a duckpin. Billy was waiting in the wings—heard the whole thing--- found out about his true mother and then let Lester have it."

Harry turned to Marino: "So there you have it detective. The whole story in a nutshell. Now what I need to know is who gets charged with what? I have a busy social summer season coming up and if I need to allow for court or..." he coughed delicately and let the thought drift off.

Mario replied: "Well, obviously this all has to be brought to the attention of the DA---but quite frankly I don't know how interested he'll be in dredging up a 40 year old murder unless, that is, the family is a driving force. We'll definitely be in touch. Let's leave it like that."

Marino and Dart left Harry sitting alone at the table with a half bottle of champagne and a cigarette perched in the ashtray. Looking back briefly at him before leaving the room, Dart had mixed feelings about the good old days of duckpin bowling. Maybe the good old days weren't as great as everyone always tried to work them up to be.....

Back in the police cruiser, Dart was silent as they drove along. Marino finally turned and asked: "What's on your mind?"

Dart said: "I guess Billy's on my mind. How could he have fooled everyone for so long?"

Marino replied: "I don't think he fooled his brother. I think Bobby was trying to cover all this and protect him. Little did he know that he was going to be one of Billy's marks."

"After getting away with three murders, pushing a fourth, he was too smart to get caught. Why did he let himself get caught?"

Marino didn't reply for a minute then said: "I think he wanted to get caught. After you kill your twin, where do you go from there?"

Epilogue

The three months since Billy's arrest for the murders of Lester Holmes, Orv Haskins, and his twin brother, Bobby Blaze, among a list of other offences, had brought a lot of change. For starters, Dart had indeed been named executrix of Mabel's trust fund for duckpin bowling. It had been a small boon to her finances and allowed her more time to work on the duckpin research. Park Canby still had every intention on keeping the project going which now dovetailed nicely with Mabel's intentions.

Enough players had complained to the head office in Boston about Dennys Smith showing more loyalty to Cal Lombard than to the leagues. He had been booted out of his position and the Congress had begun to restructure its empire. Dart had ran into Dennys on the street one day and he had informed her that it had been his choice to leave the Congress. Cal Lombard had supposedly offered him management of his casino, "just a little place", down in the Bahamas. Dart knew better but let Dennys save face where he felt he needed to.

As for Cal Lombard, he had covered his tracks as well or better than Marino had suspected. There was no hard evidence that could be pinned on him for any of his past or current actions. He got away scot-free once again although Marino had mentioned to Dart that "My sources tell me Cal has gone down to the Bahamas for an extended break" so apparently his business dealings in Baltimore were on hold. Like Harry Dingle had said at one point about Cal: "He's been doing it his whole life." Harry, despite his fears, was not implicated in any of the possible charges.

Miss Ivy had been placed at Springfield Hospital for evaluation. She had never recognized the crimes she had committed. Dart had gone to visit her once but could not stomach the complete denial she was in. She had not returned. Despite her resoluteness about her role in the events that had taken place, Miss Ivy's spirit was broken without her two "boys" around. She was becoming a shadow of her former self.

Citylanes was scheduled for a foreclosure auction. Cal's plan to sell the parts to the Phillipines had apparently fallen through. It broke Dart's heart to drive by and see the huge foreclosure sticker on the building. People talked at Ivanhoe's about trying to buy it together but it was a long shot. Several folks had approached Dart about somehow finagling some of Mabel's money to keep Citylanes afloat but Dart had figured out any loopholes to do this. Not that there wasn't enough money for it in her endowment. Unbeknowst to anyone, Mabel's humble lifestyle had disguised a huge fortune that she amassed dabbling in stocks. Her initial pot of funds had been gained from an insurance pay-out from a medical reaction to some drugs she had been given. She had been savvy enough to manipulate the funds at the right time and developed a small fortune. She had never had a family and any relatives were distant so she had turned to the big love of her life, duckpin bowling, when it came time to make a will.

The knock on the door cut into Dart's attention.

"Come in," she bellowed.

Marino strolled in and planted himself in Dart's visitor chair. "So, Miss Executrix, how does it feel to be in the seat of power?"

Dart looked up from her rosewood desk with its inlaid design and grinned. "It feels good."

Dart had been able to decorate her office to her taste---rich hues of wooded tones with some splashes of color. One of those splashes sat in the corner of the room and to the observer may have seemed out of place with the rest of the room's accoutrements. It was a chest of drawers that had some of its original paint on (a buttercup yellow color) and some stripped off. Marino was one of those observers: "What the hell's that?" he said pointing to the chest.

"Oh just one of life's challenges I guess you could say," Dart answered him. "So what are you doing in the neighborhood? Got a new case or something? I'm sure it can't compete with the last."

"It happens that I get over this way now and again. And...I thought the executrix might like to grab some lunch with me at the market."

"The sausage lady?"

"You got it."

"Let's go."